RUTH & PEN

RUTH & PEN

Emilie Pine

HAMISH HAMILTON
an imprint of
PENGUIN BOOKS

HAMISH HAMILTON

UK | USA | Canada | Ireland | Australia
India | New Zealand | South Africa

Hamish Hamilton is part of the Penguin Random House group of companies
whose addresses can be found at global.penguinrandomhouse.com.

First published 2022

004

Copyright © Emilie Pine, 2022

The moral right of the author has been asserted

Heart by Nguyen Van Sao from thenounproject.com.
Plane by trang5000 from thenounproject.com.

Set in 12.6/15.4 pt Fournier MT Std
Typeset by Jouve (UK), Milton Keynes
Printed and bound in Great Britain by Clays Ltd, Elcograf S.p.A.

The authorized representative in the EEA is Penguin Random House Ireland,
Morrison Chambers, 32 Nassau Street, Dublin D02 YH68

A CIP catalogue record for this book is available from the British Library

HARDBACK ISBN: 978–0–241–39366–6
TRADE PAPERBACK ISBN: 978–0–241–57329–7

www.greenpenguin.co.uk

for Ronan

6.19 am

Here she is.

Ruth wakes with a full bladder, still half in a dream of being somewhere else. Where was it she had been, but no, work out where *this* is. Monday morning. Home. With the other side of the bed empty.

In the bathroom she flicks on the light, sits to pee, and automatically checks her underwear. No blood. Silent thanks. She will report this at the hospital later. All fine! Only a check-up! It's not so easy to quell the fear though. Maybe she should go back to bed for a few last moments, it's still early enough. But she has that sticky after-feeling of a feverish night. May as well shower.

She dips down to make sure the plug is out and there is a rush of dizziness, a clouding.

'Is this what you want?' he had asked last night, almost as they were hanging up. And Ruth had thought, what if I tell the truth? Perhaps, though, he wasn't really asking. Perhaps he didn't want to know the answer. She cannot, now, even remember his intonation. 'Is this what you want?' Was it a question or an accusation?

The pipes make that little groaning noise before the water starts, a recriminating pause – she was meant to arrange a boiler service, dear god let it not break on her watch. Ruth steps under the water, feels the first flush of heat on her skin.

But the question will not leave her. Perhaps she should turn the shower off, get out, undo it all, phone Aidan back? She imagines herself asking him, 'What did you mean when you said the thing about *wanting*?' But he is probably still asleep, he can sleep through anything, noise, emotional turmoil, you name it he has slept, is sleeping, through it. It is one more fact in her case against him, that he is a good sleeper.

Shampoo twice, that's a thing she does now, once with the cheap stuff, once with the lemongrass. Sometimes she gives herself a blast of cold water at the end. But this morning, Ruth turns the heat up, hoping to melt the anxiety knotted in her chest.

Water off, fan still whirring. Perhaps her neighbour on the other side of the wall, quite a thin wall really, hears it, hears her, knows her? The intimacies, the rhythms of someone else's life revealed through the click of switches. Pull the shower curtain back, shake yourself, step onto the mat. 'We're self-domesticating animals,' he'd said once, early on, and she'd resisted this at the time, wanting something more than an image of a herd of cows shooing themselves into a byre, romantic love should bring something better to mind. And now, here they are: undomesticating.

The towel snags a little on the door hook, loop it up, pull it down, wrap yourself, try to remember what he said before the wanting part? Something about how she 'did not consider at all . . .' She had tuned out, though, before the full onslaught (a protective instinct), so she cannot now say exactly what it was she did not consider, though she can make a fair guess, of course. The point is, she considers a lot, too much. Back in the bedroom, glance at the clock, still not even seven, rest on the side of the bed, just for a moment. It wasn't surprising, really, that she hadn't taken in what he was saying.

He had not come home. He had not come home, that was the thing. Sunday morning had come and gone and at midday all she'd got was a text saying: DELAYED. Anything could have happened.

Ruth should get dressed, dry her hair, pull herself together. But she feels marooned on the edge of the bed. Their bed. Her bed. First client at half eight. It always seems like a good idea when you're writing it into your diary: Monday morning, 8.30 session. Like, yes, that will give me a good start to the week. Now it feels like one more act of sabotage. Some threads on the towel (a wedding present) hanging loose, she picks at one. Feet frozen and yet she does not move. '*Sirena*,' he used to call her, as she lay in their sex sheets or curled around the duvet, when he was clean and out of the shower before her. 'My *sirena*, time to get up.' The radio news clicks on. 'Good morning, it's seven o'clock on Monday, October the seventh . . .' Perhaps this is what she gets for liking herself. It had always been her mother's refrain, 'Oh, somebody likes themselves,' as if diagnosing a slip in moral judgement. Is that what she has done, liked herself too much, slipped up, driven Aidan away?

Ruth should think of clothes, but she has no clothes for who she is meant to be today. Counsellor. Patient. Wife. Wife? She stands, a monumental achievement. Her right hip is stiff, knuckles massage the part where the edge is – is there something wrong with it? With the bone, the socket, the joint? Or is this just what her body does now, at forty-three? Swing the wardrobe door open, make a choice. To run. Or to stay. Or just which jacket to wear, Ruth, *no need to make everything a production*.

Last night, when he'd finally rung, he'd told her the sales conference had ended on Saturday. But he'd found himself,

3

he said — as if he couldn't help it somehow — *found* himself
extending his booking. So, not delayed. 'They had the room
available,' he said. Ruth looks in the mirror, sees her still-
creased face, sees her body in the navy suit, thinks, oh, this
is who I am. But the thought is drowned by the roar of the
hairdryer.

Downstairs, a glance at the clock shows not enough time
for breakfast, but she can't face it anyway, as if the milk might
curdle in her. 'You're not easy,' Aidan had said, and she had
been unable to answer, suffused with anger — or was it sadness? 'I don't know how I feel,' she'd managed. 'Isn't that
your job?' he'd said.

Ruth's bag is packed, she hauls on her coat, checks keys
and wallet, pulls the front door behind her. The October air
meets her skin, damp, cold. Check the sky. Two minutes less
light each day until December. Did she lock the door? She
goes back to check. Locked, of course. The garden gate is
stiff, she should oil it or spray some stuff on it, whatever you
did. The square is still quiet, dormant looking. They joke
about it being called a square when there's only three sides.
'Brighton Triangle,' Ruth has joked how many times? Had
she ever really sounded that smug? Liking herself, her ori-
ginal sin.

But then, Ruth rounds the corner, you might as well like
yourself, since you're the only person you move through life
with. Even if you got married, even if you stood in front of a
room full of people, though not her mother, who could not be
persuaded, even if you stood there and said — promised — that
you would always be together, the reality is different. You
have yourself and that is it. Empty side of the bed proof of
that.

She's on the main road now, the sound of traffic, the sight of other people on the street, the whiff of coffee from the new place beside the Office Supplies shop. Like all her senses switching on. Only seven-something, but the cars are tailing back. Three people waiting at the bus stop, Ruth crosses at the lights, takes her place in the queue.

It's not like she hasn't asked the question herself. Is this what I want?

The truth is: No.

The truth is: Yes.

7.10 am

Two girls kissing on Instagram. *Duae puellae osculantur.* What does it mean (sustaining or draining?) if it makes you feel something warm but also makes you anxious? If you love someone does that definitely mean kissing? And what happens if one person wants to kiss and the other wants to do it only in their head? Or they want to do it in reality but they're afraid of what will happen if someone touches their face?

Pen shouldn't check her phone before she's even got up, it always makes her feel like this, kind of deathly, and she doesn't want that today, today will be the best day. It's not like the girls in the picture are really together, it's all a fake, an ad for something, the jeans maybe, and you're meant to think it's happy so then you'll want to buy the exact same outfit. There are so many things you have to think of from just one thing. (Each post is apparently worth 4g of carbon, which is draining. But then online is sustaining because she is better at online than Real Life.) It isn't like flying, though. One flight, even just to England, is basically too much carbon to imagine. And over a lifetime, how many flights? Draining. Unless they make air fuel out of hydrocarbons, that would reduce it, but it would still cost something. Every time you do anything, something is dying. She taps the heart on the screen to like it (one of the girls is a redhead), and that's another 0.2g of carbon so she has killed something. Sorry.

6

Pen lies under the weighted blanket, eyeing the blackout blind, thinking about putting one foot out, maybe getting up, but that requires more, a different kind of energy. She might find a way to make something not kill something. If she lies here, holding her breath, is she neutral? (People say, 'Don't hold your breath,' as if the fear of asphyxiating automatically outweighs the need for hope.) The air is tight in Pen's lungs, until she remembers that today will be a good day and the air comes out in a rush.

Today she will take Alice's hand and maybe she won't even need to speak, maybe the gesture will be enough, they've held hands before, but that seems so innocent now, back before they were . . . (What are they?) Anyway, Pen is so grateful, that's the word she feels, just to stand with her, so grateful to be asked, so grateful that someone picked her. That Alice picked her. Today it will all go right. They'll meet as arranged, and then have the whole day together. Pen has booked the tickets for later (a concert!) but Alice only knows there's a surprise; the feeling this gives Pen is inexpressible, it's a thrill running through her body, and she will take Alice's hand and say the things she wants to say too, she won't let what other people think matter, today the words will flow, forged by, driven by, love and aspiration, which means both breath (*spiritus*) and hope (*spero*).

No noise from the other room. Soraya isn't up yet either. Pen risks looking at her phone again, 7.30, her mum will be banging on the ceiling with the brush handle soon, it's always better to be up before that. There's a picture of that singer, she could wear baggy clothes, the clothes are ugly (even Pen knows this), but the girl in them is so light, light pours from her, she can pretend to be ugly. It's annoying how these

7

pictures make you want to be someone else. 'She probably has to wear a ton of make-up to cover up the spots and the dark circles and you are yourself, Pen, you are lovely just as you are, look at how strong you are.' Her mum is always saying things like that. 'This house is not a hotel,' that's another favourite, which is so obvious. How cool it would be to stay in a hotel and watch movies and order room service. Her and Alice maybe. Or just her.

Pen hugs her knees to her chest, lying on her side, face slipping off the pillow onto the mattress, and she remembers how she had lain like this that night and Alice, amazingly beautiful Alice, had lain down next to Pen, arms around her from behind, but only gently, and had stroked her arm, pushed her face into Pen's back, whispered so gently that Pen wondered had it really been words or just thoughts moving between them. Alice's fingers had paused on her arm, and reached a little, just a little, forward, until the tips, just the tips, of three digits had rested on Pen's right breast. Alice had whispered that they could pretend it was just the two of them in the world, and they had lain like that, Pen not moving, just holding her breath (*do* hold your breath). She should have turned to her then, Alice was so brave and Pen had said nothing, done nothing, then it had changed, something had shifted, Pen felt it, and it was just a hug again. But for a moment there had been something, she knows there had, and it is a fact: she had been held.

Pen sits up, the blanket falls back, today will be the day, they have the whole day for the longest, most perfect date in the world. She pulls the blind up, and no rain, that's a good sign. Hurry to the bathroom to claim it before Soraya. In the shower, Pen soaps everywhere, passing her hand over her soft

8

and smooth skin, lightly touching where the bumps can still be felt. It's still healing, that's what the doctor said, and if Pen puts vitamin E oil on, soon no one will even notice. Pen thinks that if she really heals it will be because someone else touches her, touches the raised lines that run in neat rows along the soft pink flesh of her thighs.

Pen shuts off the hot water, how are you meant to stick to three minutes? Dutifully she squeegees the walls (this house is not a hotel). Maybe she should use her mother's expensive cream on her face? It says 'glow' on the jar, and it might make Alice see her the way she sees Alice. A glow. Aglow. Pen wipes the glass with her hand. It's weird when you look in the mirror, you see your face the way no one else does, you look into your own eyes. Pen wonders if this means you know how you look better than anyone else does, better in this case meaning more accurate but perhaps also better? Or worse? Meaning both. Pen has a no-selfie policy because her eyes are not where they're meant to be in the photos, her whole face is somehow out of alignment, that's not what I look like, she wants to say. Her mother tells her not to worry so much, that 'no one is looking at you, Pen'. Secretly, very secretly, Pen fears she is vain (and also, everyone *is* looking at her). *Ecce! In pictura est puella.* It's how every story begins.

'It's what's on the inside that counts,' her mother chants over and over, saying things like 'mirror tax', because these-days-young-women have all their ambition sapped just by basically fighting-off-all-the-negative-messaging. Pen's mother talks like this, in speeches sometimes. It comes of being a lecturer. And she has rules, too, about looking at things online, about texting other people when you're with someone, mealtimes are quality time, as if time has different qualities – good or bad, it passes at exactly the same rate. Actually, that is not a fact. Time runs faster the higher the altitude so that if Pen is upstairs and her mother is downstairs, her time is faster or more compressed or something than her mother's, but who is to say which is the better quality? What is on the inside isn't the right thing to say, anyway, because what if what's on the inside is even more different? That's another thing Pen can't say, can only think, because if she says it out loud she'll get a long talk on everyone-is-different. Obviously, thinks Pen, rolling her eyes when she gets that particular lecture.

Different is like special, one of those words that people say with a kind of emphasis that makes them think they're being tactful. 'Just say what you actually mean,' Pen wants to shout, only then people would tell her she was over-excited. At least the woman-therapist agrees. And at least she understands that what Pen needs is not so much a label, as strategies to calm the world's chaos. Okay, then, the woman-therapist says. Feel the triggers, Pen. Feel them, Name them, Know them. Look at your hands, because that'll give you a sense of control. When people talk to you, don't look at their faces, too much stimulus. When your brain has too much in it, work out which it is, thinking or feeling? What is the feeling? Positive, negative, neutral? Pen has made observation her ally. Pen used to just call her 'the woman' because having to go to a therapist was basically proof that she was not like other girls, but then her mother said, 'Come on, Pen, don't fall for that old shame trick.' Because her mother has a therapist too. So Pen came up with her own label.

Pen's room is difficult, it doesn't take much observation to know that. It's either totally tidy or totally messy and today is messy, which makes getting in the door hard because she has to step over and around things and that's complicated. She should keep it tidy but just because you should do something doesn't mean you do it and sometimes she feels like shouting that none of the rules, even if she follows all of them, will mean she's not going to get knotted up or freeze or bump into things. Pen had actually said this in a session and the woman-therapist had paused and it sounded like she was laughing but obviously not because that was against the rules, and then she said, 'Oh Pen, it's so normal, you're just a teenager.' So that Pen felt better and allowed herself one door slam when she got home and afterwards, at dinner, her mother had said, 'What was that all about?' but didn't freak out. None of which helps Pen right now because everything is everywhere, so she just takes her cool-date-outfit from the chair and the fabric is soft and smooth against her skin, which makes her feel instantly better. The floor thumps, which is the ceiling for her mother, and whatever the speed of time, it's time to go down.

Crash goes the dish, crunch goes the toast, and Pen winces as the water pump grinds because it is so much worse when other people make noise. 'You'll be careful today,' Claire says. Claire is Pen's mother and she means well and wants to keep her safe but she doesn't want her to go, Pen knows, because she doesn't understand. Pen is doing it for love.

'There may be some – you know, not everyone will be there necessarily for the same reasons as you are, and it'll be loud.'

Pen just concentrates on the line of little pills on the table, on the feeling of yellow cereal softening in her mouth.

'You can leave any time you want to,' Claire persists, because her daughter hates noise, hates people around her, prefers to be by herself, is perfectly happy by herself in fact, so hundreds of people on a demonstration will be hard. Claire would fight anyone to the death who said her daughter shouldn't be allowed to do some things, but she also wishes she could keep her at home sometimes. 'I mean, the climate is important, I just wish you were going to school—'

'CLAIRE!'

Well, at least it's a response. Pen had made the day off sound like a civics lesson and Claire is familiar with the strikes, excusing students from her own classes on Fridays, but this is a Monday and Pen is in fifth year, it doesn't really matter that she's better at English than her teacher practically, turning up is important, and Claire knows there are different ways to learn, but it's doubtful the geography exam will include a section on Extinction Rebellion.

Even Pen, when she stops to think about it, feels the threat of exams looming, a kind of fear at the bottom of her stomach. But then that's what every day feels like.

Bang! Most of the noise comes from the smallest person. Soraya is making a bid for attention. Pen can't see her, doesn't look up from studying the milk in the bowl, the few floating flakes (rumour has it there's more salt in a bowl of these than in seawater), but she hears her shuffle and whine and breathe too loudly. She's asking for an apple now, 'for school'. She doesn't even like apples, Pen thinks, but then as Claire reaches for the fridge door, rustling the bags as she pulls the apple out, and Pen imagines pushing her sister so she's out of her face, she feels Soraya lean close to her and whisper, 'Have a good time today.' Pen is so surprised she looks up at Soraya's beatific smile. It is the O'Neill family yo-yo effect, christened by Sandy, that just at the point you start thinking, this can't be my family, they're driving me crazy, one of them will turn round and do or say something to make you feel amazing.

And suddenly today is going to be good again, Pen feels it in her bones. Her mother puts an apple on the table in front of her body.

'Stack the dishwasher, put away last night's dry dishes, do *something* with your bedroom because it's a total disaster, Pen, and this isn't a hotel.' Claire has decided she may as well get some housework out of her daughter, she's fishing in her bag, coat in hand, 'Here's something for today,' the money on the table. 'Make sure you eat, wear your mac, I don't care if it's not cool, you don't want to catch a flu.' Pen nods. 'You could say something once in a while.' Claire sounds like she's annoyed, although she's not – it was meant to come out funny.

But Pen raises her head, looks over at her mother, and then lifts her hands and shimmies them in the air. Soraya has her hands up now and Claire too, an unbreakable circle. The O'Neill women. 'Have a good day, I'll see you for Monday-night-pizza.' The front door bangs, the walls shake a little.

Today Pen will not shake, today the words will come, today she will take Alice's hand.

7.23 am

'Good morning to you!' the voice says, and Ruth looks up and thinks, what now / oh no / where is the bus? Because she does not want to talk, is not able to, but it's Stephen, and it must be years, they had known each other in school. He really is very tall. Ruth feels suddenly aware of her make-up-less face.

'You're solving the nation's problems,' Stephen says, and this throws Ruth because what is he talking about? And then it becomes apparent he means the radio phone-in and how does he know, isn't he working abroad?

'Mm, it's good, lots of problems,' she says, sounding like an idiot. 'It's challenging,' she says, trying to claim back some ground but losing it again with a jumbled thought. 'Aren't you in Australia?'

'I'm back to sell my apartment,' Stephen gestures with a hand towards Terenure Cross. 'Want to buy a place out there . . . and I can check in from the Dublin office, though the time difference is a bit tricky.'

Ruth just nods.

'I'm on my way to the gym, actually,' he raises the kitbag for proof. 'I'm not waiting for the bus. Just a bystander, or bywalker, ha ha.'

Ruth's neck is sore from being bent back, she tries to make her glance at the display subtle. It still says 1 MIN / 1 NÓM. Come now, come now, she wills it.

'I've enjoyed following you,' he says, and then, remarkably, 'I have your voice in my ears.' Stephen smiles, and when she still looks blank, he actually points to the side of his head, as if she didn't get the concept of ear. 'Podcast,' he says finally.

'Oh. Weird,' Ruth says, because what, really, do you say to that?

'Is everything,' Stephen's face looks puzzled, 'is everything okay, Ruth?'

'Monday morning,' Ruth says, feeling the flicker of panic. She does not say, *and my husband did not come home.*

'Manic Monday, of course!' Stephen's smile is broad as he shakes his head at another week starting. The sound of a louder engine, the bus arriving. 'Good luck with your day, then. Maybe we could catch up some evening before I go?'

'Great!' Ruth gives him an awkward half-wave, she is already at the step, and as she glances back, nodding (they both know they will not catch up), she thinks that his grin looks a little forced.

Ruth taps her card, and going up the stairs thinks of that night, someone's twenty-first. She and Stephen had seen each other and next thing they were hugging, drunkenly, amazedly confessing how much they'd liked each other in school but had been too shy, and that night felt different, no inhibitions, it was all laid out for them, their exciting lives to be, and they had talked and kissed in the park, he helping her over the railings and suddenly it had been dawn and both of them in his bed. God, the next day! Ruth was not good with hangovers. Stephen had texted, and at first it was all romantic and xx after his name, but then it turned out he had an on-again-off-again, but now on, definitely-on girlfriend. Ruth was going travelling anyway. She grimaces, remembering how real it had all seemed.

The bus crawls through Harold's Cross, Ruth can practically feel herself ageing. Had it been, back then, the freest time of her life? The hours, the days they'd wasted had felt luxurious, oh yes. But at the time, was it really so wonderful? Did it feel free? Ruth almost winces. It was all possible, that's what everyone had said to her. 'It's all ahead of you.' They meant well, but it all being possible felt almost the same as none of it being.

Ruth opens the tiny compact. Suspiciously she looks at the image, how to make herself look like a normal person? Okay then, scribble on your face with the crayon that promises brightening, buff with powder. Clamp the compact and mascara tube in one hand, stab at your lashes with the wand in the other. Shit, nearly dropped it. Hold the mirror back to judge the effect. Ruth dabs some pink on her cheeks. Pointless really, it all feels pointless. Isn't it absurd, anyway, to take red out of one part of your face only to add it to another?

The bus jerks in short bursts onto Clanbrassil Street, smarter now – the abattoir gone, the old houses knocked down when she was a child to make way for the new bus lanes, and it did make things quicker into town. Ruth can feel the pull of her mother's house, she could see it if she craned, Lombard Street. Someone else's house now, the wisteria still growing over the door. She won't look for it, what is it, only a house.

Past St Patrick's, then Christ Church ahead at last. A final survey in the mirror before Ruth gathers it all into her bag and goes down. The bus veers past the cathedral, where her friends sing at Christmas, the annual genuflection, songs and candles. Past the Lord Edward pub on the corner. Is there still sawdust on the floor of the bar? Or maybe that was only ever in her imagination? They shudder to a halt.

Off the bus, and the air still feels like rain, though the sky is brighter. Ruth turns left at Cow's Lane, she usually likes this invented street, with its yoga and tattoos and plants and books. When was the last time she read a book? That was freedom, really, not time to waste, but time to do the things you wanted. The back of the theatre, and all these lanes, all these alleys, had been forgotten. Strange to think this was once the centre of the city, right up to the castle, the heart of things. That's what a few hundred years did for you, moved the boundaries. The little shop where she'd bought her mother those cashmere gloves one Christmas, 'Made in Ireland' the label said, but it was too much to hope for that woman's approval. The memorial to the Magdalen Laundries on the corner which on other days, days that are not today, makes Ruth feel sick to think about, because her life was one long freedom, really. Today, though, she walks past, unaware.

Widening out onto Parliament Street, she glances back at the pub she'd worked in all through college, the years when there were only a few places men could hold hands. Grattan Bridge. Waiting at the lights, Ruth thinks of Aidan and, damn it, because she was doing so well. 'These,' he'd said, stopping her one day as they were crossing, pointing at the metalwork along the bridge, 'look at these – they're sea horses.' He'd explained that they were a sign of loyalty, because they mate for life. They are also unique, she wants to tell him now, having looked them up afterwards, for the male sea horse being the one to bear the unborn young.

Capel Street, named for someone, an earl maybe? It seems

some distance from that now, with all its soup and sushi and bibimbap. Strange, Ruth thinks, pausing at a shopfront, how you can smell the scent of olives or spices and the fact that your husband possibly/maybe/probably hates you can be pushed aside, put almost out of mind, at the prospect of food. Ruth nods to the woman behind the counter as she enters the shop. (Greek? Turkish? Is it rude not to know?) 'Yes, those,' the man ahead says, pointing to a tray of pistachio-topped baklava. The woman serves him and smiles at Ruth, who nods again to show she can wait.

The pastry is warm in her hand and the oil is coming through the paper bag already. Ruth curls the edge down to bite into it. She walks up the street (her street, she claims it) allowing herself to savour her pastry, crispy, salty, cheesy. Borek. She can feel her feet on the pavement and the warmth through the paper and the slip of oil on her lips, and all of these things mean that she might just make it through today.

Ruth lets herself into the narrow hallway. Dim, quiet, she must be the first in. She picks up the circulars for pizza and massages, piles them on the shelf, climbs the stairs, up up up. All efficiency now she flicks on lights, pushes boost on the heat, always colder after the weekend, turns on her desk light. Home, in a way. She goes out to the kitchen, fills the kettle, gets down a mug, quite a mishmash, they should sort out the cupboards, measures the coffee into the cafetière, listens to the growing boil of the water, watches for the light to click off. Teaspoon in the sink, she can wash it later. Deal with everything later. Ruth takes her mug next door, hovering over her desk, taking out the folder of notes, glancing through. The page shows her handwriting, her typed comments, all in order. Yes, she knows who this person is. Plump a cushion, move the box of tissues closer to the chair. Pause. There is time.

'You must hear some interesting stories?' It was their first date. Aidan had looked genuinely interested, was that it, was that why she had wanted to confess to him? That she felt inadequate in the face of the suffering people trusted her with. She'd said instead that she was amazed (is still amazed) at how much energy is taken up with feeling bad about ourselves. Had told him that, details aside, almost everyone's pain is the same. Then she'd stopped, aware of the distance between what she felt and what she was saying. Later, Aidan told her this reticence – shyness he'd called it – had been charming, and she had said nothing then, either, to correct his false impression. Aidan. They were not sea horses.

The door chime goes. Turn away from the window, go to the wall, press the button. Ruth hears the echo of a voice, speaks, buzzes Anthony in. She has a minute now because Anthony will take the stairs slowly, he hates to arrive out of breath, and Ruth exhales again to clear her mind, to settle herself, to make herself ready to listen, to draw a line between her life and this other.

8.01 am

The cutlery goes with points and tines up. Pen rearranges
them by type, knives together, forks together, spoons on the
other side. There is a feeling inside your head when things
are in order. Empty-headed means unintelligent, but what joy
would it be to have an actually empty head, to not have the
echoes of stupid people saying that you're broken jangling
around inside. Pen asked the woman-therapist in their very
first session if talking was the only way to get things out of her
head? The woman-therapist said that a) Pen is right, she's not
broken, and therefore she is not in need of fixing, b) wouldn't
it be great if the world could be made to suit everyone, and
c) that no one has to talk if they don't want to. So sometimes
they just sit quietly and that, in a way, is like having an empty
head.

'What does a full head feel like?' That was a question the
woman-therapist had asked her. Pen had just shaken her head,
so the woman-therapist asked her to come the next week with
some words written down and they'd get there slowly. When
you find the right words it's as if they make the world come
into focus, but when Pen tried to find words for the feelings
on the inside of her head it was like standing in front of a wall
of words. So that by the morning of her next appointment,
Pen still hadn't thought of the right thing to say, or even write
down. She'd taken one of her mum's poetry books instead,

Dickinson, with golden lettering on the spine. When she got to the room, she opened it at the page and held it up for show.

I felt a Funeral, in my Brain

And the woman-therapist said, 'Is this whole thing how you feel?' and Pen nodded and then the woman-therapist asked her to say which lines felt the most like how she felt. Pen pointed to the first line and then, when she realised she was meant to say something else, she slowly read out:

A Service, like a Drum –
Kept beating – beating – till I thought
My mind was going numb –

The woman-therapist nodded again, and Pen realised that she'd finally found someone who listened properly. Then the woman-therapist explained that thinking of things – like thinking you should do something, or wondering what other people thought of you, or wondering if your mum was okay – each of those thoughts was like opening a file in your brain. And the more thoughts you had, the more your brain filled up with open files, which flashed and clicked to remind your brain that they were there. So if you had a lot of 'active thoughts', the woman-therapist said, it was like your brain being filled with flashing lights and clicking noises. And that was enough to send anyone into panic mode.

Pen rinses the bowls and the water-feeling on her hand is kind of soothing, which is why she chose this chore. Bowls in the upper rack, starting at the back so that the weight of them doesn't drag the hinges too much. The therapy room is calm and quiet and kind of blank, which Pen likes now that she's been going long enough to relax and look around her more. Pen sits opposite the woman-therapist, which is also opposite the window, so she can see sky through the window, and because they are high up she sees the tops of the buildings across the road, a roofscape (if Pen ever writes a poem, it will include the word 'scape'). When she is there, in the room, and the woman-therapist explains that there are strategies for turning off the flashing lights in your brain, for making things feel calm, they all make sense and Pen nods and says thank you at the end and goes home. Last week she'd told the woman-therapist about the protest and the date with Alice, and she'd said she was calm about it. But today it feels more complicated. What if people won't give her space, or there's too much shouting? Because too often other people don't wait for her to take a breath and find her bearings, they just don't want to wait. Once, when Pen had had a bad week, the woman-therapist told her she would be okay because she has two things in her favour: she's resourceful and she has agency. Then she said that neurodiverse people are often highly successful or creative because they have this resourcefulness, all these coping strategies for Real Life, that they take tasks methodically or differently from everyone else. That they get shit done. She had said that, '*shit*', and Pen had smiled, because it was like something Alice would say.

There are glasses you have to wash by hand, like this one, made of a kind of green glass, which has a bubble inside the base and is heavy. Pen is careful picking it up from the drainer, turning it inside the cloth to catch any last drops of water. She slides it gently onto the higher shelf. It was a wedding present for her parents and there was a set of six originally. Now there's just this one so you have to be extra particular with it.

Pen calls her dad Sandy, but he doesn't like her to use his name like that – when she does, he pauses and says, 'Excuse me?' Sometimes he calls her Penelope and she won't respond, or she calls him Mr O'Neill the next time, which he hates even more, so there are two of them in it, Claire says. Sandy is a roads engineer. He wanted to be an architect, but people don't always get their first choice, which Sandy-sorry-Dad seemed to think was an important life lesson but Claire-aka-Mum thought was 'a bit defeatist, actually'. 'Whatever,' shrugs Pen when they get like that. Sandy is interested in buildings, in how they look or don't look. 'Uninspiring,' he says every Saturday when he picks them up, looking at the house with narrowed eyes, as if it's the nondescript street he doesn't want and not them. Pen knows that the things people say aren't always about you, that instead they show you how the other person feels on the inside. Pen thinks of the way words touch the surface of things, sliding across the world and your tongue. Some words can make you feel loved and soft, and others dent and damage.

Did the builders or designers find it uninspiring? Pen wonders if they were disappointed, if all the people that it took to create even one house had tried to make something that would make others feel inspired? Or did they just want to make the occupants feel sheltered? But Pen does not shudder the way Claire does when Sandy says things like that, or things about 'this country', she does not say, 'What's so great about being from England?' Mostly, Pen just listens, because she likes looking at buildings too, and she likes imagining the lives inside, and she likes it, basically, when Sandy talks to her at all.

After her parents split up, the noise and the anxiety got really bad, and even though Pen didn't like school she would ask her teachers if she could stay late and read in the classroom, but she couldn't because of insurance or something. She had to come home and even if only her mum and Soraya were there it was still like you could hear the noise, so then Pen would refuse to leave her room (which was also Soraya's room, which meant Soraya would start shouting because Pen-always-gets-what-she-wants-it's-my-room-too). Then they moved and the noise got less. And then she started going to therapy. 'It's only half an hour,' her mum said because Pen didn't want to go at first, but then it became the best half-hour of the week, it was funny the way that could happen (funny-strange). The therapy room has chairs that are far enough apart that you don't have to touch and if you look over the other person's shoulder it doesn't look rude, it just looks like you are being thoughtful. And then the woman-therapist asks her questions and when Pen answers it is like a weight lifts from her chest (which is a metaphor but also it feels real). It's good to be her, is what the woman-therapist mostly says, hard sometimes but good.

Pen thinks about the timetable. Transport, check. Meeting, check. Rally, check. March, check. After that, Pen's not sure, but she and Alice will probably hang out until the concert. Pen has a lot of places marked on her phone map so that they can go for food or a walk. She'd wanted to ask Claire what was cool to do in town but that seemed like an uncool thing to do when you were sixteen, asking your mum, so she'd looked it up instead and that had made her remember going to see the bog bodies in the museum and the Viking gold. Maybe she can take Alice there, though she's not sure if Alice will want to look at bodies from 400 BCE that were basically just from the Midlands. The first time she saw them, Pen looked at the bodies with skin like darkest brown leather and fingernails and fingerprints and hair and thought, we are the same, we feel the same, even across thousands of years. Will Alice think that too? Museums probably don't count as cool or romantic though. ('Draining or sustaining, Pen?' the woman-therapist asks, because she is always urging Pen to actively choose what's best.) But maybe Alice, even though she likes-her-for-her, doesn't need to know that Pen prefers to be in a museum than on a street? Maybe she'll text and ask her? She's going to walk on the edge today anyway, she'd reminded Alice in a text last night. Pen loves texting, which is talking without faces, basically. Sometimes, when she's stuck, she wishes she could just hold up emoji signs.

Pen checks her phone because she should see what is happening in the world, because it's no good just going on marches. You need to know the facts. She has to search deliberately these days for stuff about the Amazon fires – last month it was everywhere but now the top stories are all invasion and borders, refugees rather than fires, though they are basically the same story. The world is burning. Not that you would know from the media, Pen scrolls for ages, no real-burning-Amazon (lots of the other one).

Pen had brought up the fires with Sandy one time. They were in his apartment (uninspiring, actually) for dinner, and he'd even remembered to get her the melt-in-the-middle vegetarian burgers she likes, which automatically marked the day as unusual. 'What are you doing at school?' he asked, though it was still August and they weren't back yet. But Pen forgave him because it was hard to make conversation. 'What do you think of the rainforest fires?' she'd said, because current affairs seemed like a safe topic. 'South America, hunh?' he'd shrugged.

'You know why they do it?' Pen had given a tiny headshake. 'Where do you think all that soya comes from?' And Sandy had nodded at her burger. She was contributing (how many grams?) – that's what he was really saying. Pen wanted to tell him that his burger was worse but he'd moved on, he was teasing her sister about something now. Later that night, Claire had found her a chart online of all the greenhouse emissions of different proteins and Pen started eating more lentils because you could grow them in a drought.

'There has been a significant drop in new blazes in the forests,' says Brazil, although there are questions about how reliable these statements are, given the president is, basically, a total dictator, says Alice. But even he admits there are more fires than before, though fewer new ones, but more overall than at any time in recorded history, which is not all of history, just the bits they write down. If you don't have statistics things don't exist, says one website, though anyone can see the flaw in that one.

It's rare that Pen is in the house by herself, there's usually Claire and Soraya, or Catherine, who picks Soraya up from school, or Claire working from home. 'I can't afford to do the job-share thing,' Pen heard Claire say once, on the phone to her best friend. 'I'm just exhausted, abso-fucking-lutely exhausted.' (When you split a word like that, with another word in the middle, it's called tmesis. Tmesis is also an unusual and thus favourite word, because there should be a vowel between consonants 't' and 'm' but the vowel is left out.) Anyway, being alone is a rare pleasure for Pen. Plus, on-your-own means you can look at anything. Pen heads for the main bedroom.

She can smell her mother, her familiar, comforting, body type of smell. It smells of night. Would her mother want her to open the window? Pen wonders if her mother dreams, perhaps she's too tired, she says she's tired a lot, with a long sigh, stretching her back, or rubbing her feet, 'I'm so tired, make me a cup of tea, love.' That word, love, it slips out sometimes and Pen can't help it, give me more *SPACE*, she jerks away. But she does make the tea, at least. It is an irony, now, that she wants to say the same word to Alice, and she hopes, really hopes, that Alice will not want space. Pen is good at making tea, at warming the cup, if they had a teapot she could do it properly. But then think of the waste if they made a pot and didn't finish it. At least they've switched to loose tea (no more plastic teabags), but only because Claire said she couldn't take the nagging any more, and Pen suspects she still drinks the Barry's stuff at work.

The top drawer is underwear, some neatly rolled, a reminder of Claire's magic tidying-up phase, the rolled ones look lacy, brighter, the others a jumble. Camisoles in there too. Her mother says she wears them so she can wave her arms around during class and not get fired for flashing, but Pen would wear them for the silky, sexy feel on her skin. The word camisole is pleasing, *camisia*, Latin for nightgown or shirt. There are five people in the Latin class and Pen guesses she's not the only one using the lunchtime slot to avoid the social crush of the canteen. 'I'm taking Latin now,' she'd announced at home, back when they lived in the old house. 'Going to be a doctor, then,' said Sandy, as if it's only about jobs. Pen does not know what she wants to be ('You can't "be" something,' says Claire, 'you *do* things'), but something where there is beauty and time and space is what she wants.

The drawers aren't really that interesting, so Pen's attention turns to the wardrobe. The top shelf is too high for her mother who needs to use the bathroom stool but Pen's fingers can grasp the edge of the box, tug at the scarf that keeps it closed, pull it down towards her. There is a rattle. Remember how it was, put it back how it was, move through life carefully, Pen's fingers fumble at the knot. There are only four items inside: two rings, one necklace and a roll of notes. Pen fingers the metal, recognises the setting and the plain band. It makes sense that you can't throw these things away, that you keep them, and keep too, for a while, the ridge on your finger where they used to go. They are too small for Pen's hands. The necklace Pen has never seen before, it looks old-fashioned, gold. Pen slides off the elastic, a hair bobble, and unfurls the notes. Fifties, twelve of them. Why is there six hundred euro in the wardrobe? Pen thinks of the economising, her mother's mantra, thinks of the twenty in her pocket from this morning, and re-rolls the notes, carefully nesting them so the elastic will go back on. Is it exactly how it was? Money is a kind of dirt – if you work with money your hands are filthy at the end of the day. Money is freedom too, though. You can want to wash your hands of one, but you need the other.

Pen sits on the floor for a while, wondering what the box really means. Most of the time Claire says she is just busy getting them all through each day. Did she put the things in the box on purpose? Or in that way where you do something you don't know you're going to do? Knowing her mum, probably the first way. Pen lids the box and ties the scarf around it again, tips it onto the shelf – it's pretty much how it was as she closes the wardrobe door. Pen checks her watch. Nearly time.

8.30 am

'Are you sure you want this much detail?'

In his late fifties, Anthony is a man with a gentle appearance. Ruth has come to know the face before her, how his lips seem to disappear when he's nervous. And the way his hands twist as he's talking.

'It gives me a sense of you, to know what your day is like.'

Ruth and Anthony have covered the big subjects, death, of course.

'I used to be so vain about clothes,' Anthony says, 'but now, I can't find the energy. Weekends, like I said, I don't see anyone anyway. Jeans, a jumper. I can't think how boring this is for you.'

'Please, go on,' Ruth says.

'I go to the bathroom, do my business, go downstairs. And this moment I hate, because I have to go fast through the hall, past the living-room door, because that was his room, after the fall. I'm not, well, you can see, I'm not super-strong, physically. So he slept down there. Sometimes I'd let myself fall asleep on the sofa, you know, just to be in the same room. And I'd always kiss him, just a gentle kiss on his forehead, or his hair if he was asleep on his side.'

'He must have known he was very loved,' Ruth says as Anthony pauses. A nod shows this has landed.

'I couldn't do that so much in the hospital, well, you know

all that, because they were quite strict about visiting, depending on what nurse it was. And they kept asking me, oh, they forgot, I suppose, they kept asking if he had "another brother" who could relieve me. I can't blame them, but it was hard to have to answer it.'

Ruth nods, and when it seems he has reached a full stop, not just a pause, she prompts again. 'Did you talk about it with Michael? About his family?'

Anthony shakes his head slightly. 'I know he preferred being at home. He always loved that house, did I tell you? Yes, well. He liked the house, we both did. It had a good atmosphere, but I wish . . . Well, perhaps, that we'd bought on the other side of the street, the back is north facing, makes it very dark in the mornings. And then –'

Ruth jots down '*displacement?*' in her notebook, notices Anthony notice the gesture.

'Later on, neighbours, not the ones who'd lived there for years, but the new ones moving in since the crash, put up scaffolding and so on, remaking their houses, with light-filled this-and-that extensions. Like mini-mansions.'

Another pause comes, but this one Ruth decides to leave.

'I liked the simplicity of what we had. I would say that to him, and he'd squeeze my hand.'

'That was an important thing to say. Did you talk about your feelings more often after that?'

There is another tiny shake of Anthony's head. 'We had a good life. Write that bit down.'

'I have, don't worry,' Ruth smiles. 'Do you have other people you can talk to about him now? About the good life you had?'

'I went out for work drinks last week, I forgot to mention that. First Thursday of the month, it's a standing thing.'

'Did that feel like an important thing to do, to get back to a routine?'

'Everyone was very nice. Solicitous. But then they were talking about things I just don't care about. You can't really say, "Oh, my dead husband," every five minutes, it's kind of a downer. Do you think I should confront people, is that it?'

Ruth leaves a small gap. 'What about the friends from the hospice. Are you seeing them now?'

He glances away. Anthony can talk about death and loss without even the threat of a tear, it's kindness that sets him off.

'We actually have a picnic planned for next weekend. We're slowly doing parts of the Wicklow Way, one stage at a time. Only the weather hasn't been playing ball, so this time we're just heading to Three Rock. Gerard brings the thermos, Eimear can be relied on for interesting sandwiches. Though I think, and don't quote me on this, I think she outsources the actual making of them to the local café.' Anthony gives a fond smile. 'Sorry, you probably have one of those big extensions, Ruth, do you? I didn't mean to be rude, earlier.'

'We do,' Ruth smiles. 'Not quite "mini-mansion" level, but yes, it is very light. Are you thinking about doing that now, changing your own house?'

But this only receives a sharp headshake.

'So, then, Anthony, let's get back to your weekend – when you're not with friends, do you find it easier to be in the house now?'

'I went for brunch, actually,' he points vaguely behind him. 'There's a crêperie place near the canal, Le Petit Breton.'

Ruth nods.

'And I set myself the task of reading the whole paper. I got into the habit in the hospital, you can't really concentrate to read anything more than the paper, so I was missing it and I'd taught myself to do the sudoku, which he laughed at me for. He always held his skill with maths over me, "Honours Maths," he would say, but in fact I was always better, restaurant bills and so on. So at brunch, I had a galette and my paper and chatted a bit with the woman who runs it. And when I got home, I made myself walk into the living room. I was still wearing my coat, just standing there, and the light really was lovely. And I thought maybe I should get one of those sledgehammers and knock out the dividing wall.'

Ruth nods.

'But then I imagined him again, Michael. Not a fan of change, you see. He'd say, "Catch yourself on!" whenever I suggested something like that. And it's like, sometimes, I can hear the echo. Strange how the thing that used to drive you mad is what you miss.'

'Can you tell me a little more about that?' Ruth says.

9.51 am

The train is not for another forty-two minutes and it takes twelve minutes to walk to the station. That's thirty minutes to make sure everything is perfect. Pen has a glass of water. Pen goes to the loo. Pen looks at everything in the silent house. Pen stands and listens to the silence. And then it is only eighteen minutes until the train.

In the hall, Pen looks in the full-length mirror (*speculum* in Latin). When they'd gone shopping for jeans, Alice had said she wished her thighs were smaller, her hips narrower. Pen just sat on the stool, holding Alice's coat. Alice had pulled the sides of her legs back, trying to see what she'd look like if she could shave off the edges. 'Like this, I'd be smaller, I could wear clothes from the boys' section,' she said. Then Pen said, 'If you wear the baggy jeans no one can tell,' and Alice smiled, a real smile, not like the fake-mirror-pose one. And Pen thought *Aliciae Per Speculum Transitus* in her head and smiled back because she could see Alice and her in the mirror at the same time. Alice and Pen are giving up shopping anyway – new clothes, basically – for the environment. Pen is happy with this arrangement, she hates shopping, rails and rails of things, all different and all the same.

'You can go two ways,' Claire says. 'The world can be hard, and so you have to choose how to deal with that, hard or soft.' When Claire says things like that Pen wonders if she knows how it sounds.

Pen takes her blue and pink mac, which is definitely not cool (why didn't she get a yellow one?), but it's what's on the inside, blah blah blah. The house alarm narrates her progress, alarmed to away, thirty seconds to full alarm, she pulls the door behind her, double-locks it. She checks her travel pass, her money, her phone, and puts in her earbuds. Then she allows herself to look up. Here comes her perfect day. The walking playlist starts. It used to be whale song because that's a type of pink noise. Who knew noise had colours, but nature is full of pink noise it turns out, like rustling leaves or heartbeats. Pen likes the flat, even kind of sound and the idea that whales sing at a unique frequency. But recently she read an article about how this one whale had lost her pod and that was just way too lonely. So Pen hit shuffle and found music on an upbeat kind of frequency. And for now, that's Lizzo. Pen steps out onto the road, the pavement. No other pedestrians and the houses in their right places. Walking, head forward, Pen crosses Cross Avenue.

Pen's mother says she can live at home when she goes to college, which is cool because Chloe at school says her mother is counting the days till she moves out and she's going to turn her room into something, she doesn't care what, a yoga studio maybe. Pen doesn't really go to other people's houses, not after last year, besides, Alice lives on the other side of the city. She has to get a train to school every day, she gets the train with different people than Pen knows. It's one of the great things about Alice, everyone likes her. At first when Alice came over they just stayed in the kitchen but during the summer they started going to Pen's bedroom and now it feels normal. Alice takes off her shoes without being asked and she doesn't even say anything if the room is super-organised or super-messy, it's as if it doesn't bother her at all.

The singer sounds really confident and not lonely at all, but it's not clear how you can be your own soulmate. Pen can't imagine being so relaxed that you could sing out loud. It's okay, that's what Claire says, you don't have to keep a tally of the things you don't want to do, there's so much other stuff to be great at. Like what, Pen wants to ask, though she knows her mother will say she's great at listening, she's great at being an older sister – but Pen wants to be great at kissing and laughing out loud and marching, she really hopes she's good at that, at those, at all of them. (Is Alice already good at them?) Turning onto Marine Road, Pen reckons it would be hard to want more than one person at a time. It takes so much energy just to focus on even one person. Claire recently told her friend Jenny (also getting a divorce) that she was giving up on that for a while, anyway. Jenny was over for dinner and they'd had wine and they laughed out loud a lot. Their exes really were pieces of work.

There's no queue at the ice-cream shop because everyone else is in school. Chloe and Sarah and Lauren and Aoife. Pen's breath almost comes in short bursts when she thinks of them. They're just bitches, Alice says, but it's hard to agree when you used to want them to like you. Redirect, that's what the woman-therapist says. So Pen looks again at the ice-cream shop and thinks, what can I think of instead, perhaps she should get an ice-cream too given that she is already biting off more than she can chew, Claire would find that funny. Pen collects idioms because they are greater than the sum of their parts. At first they are confusing, idioms and metaphors, but Claire's work friend Naomi had spent a whole Sunday morning with her once explaining them, how they were one thing on the outside, but look again and they were much more interesting. Though, basically, some of them are always going to be weird, like if you want to mean, don't make the same mistake twice, you can say a burned child dreads the fire. But Claire has asked her not to use that one because it's a bit brutal, actually.

There are seventeen steps down, once Pen goes through the gate, and then she's on the platform. She walks to the far end, past the real-time signs, past the shelter, the benches, towards the signal lights. This will mean she gets off the train right at the ticket gates in town and so she is one step closer to being perfect.

Last year in Lauren's house. Just don't think about it, Alice said. Why was she even there, Sandy asked, as if it was her fault for going.

The display screen says the train is in 3 MINS. Pen checks her watch (10:30) to see if it's a real three minutes or the fake kind, which is really four or five, but they want you to think it's on schedule because everybody wants to be on schedule. Sandy used to say that Mussolini made the trains run on time, not-like-in-this-country. Claire would roll her eyes at that one, pointing out the 'disastrous privatisation of British Rail' and another fight about the differences between Ireland and England would start. But Pen thinks maybe he was trying to make a joke, basically, and it just wasn't funny (though it is funny-strange). I mean, if you think about it, she wants to say to her father, if you think about it, it's never a person but fear that makes people do things, not more efficiently, or better, but faster because when you're afraid you act in a blur. Isn't it funny-strange, Pen thinks, that you can't say words back to a person when you're with them, but their voice stays in your head, and you hear it and talk to it when they're not around.

People don't really understand fear, how bad it is. Or that's how it seems, because if they really knew, if they knew how painful fear feels, wouldn't they do everything they could to stop it? Pen thinks about this every time she has to be part of a group project or is asked to speak in class. Even though she has a special sticker on her file, there are some teachers who don't know or who don't think, or who do think and still say things like, 'It's necessary she develop-some-public-speaking-skills.' All those teachers who don't care about Pen's fear call on her in class. And then they're the ones who panic when she doesn't talk. 'The girl won't even say boo to a goose.' (One teacher said this to Claire, and Pen almost looked round for the geese.) Anyway, all the teachers, even the kind ones, think that presentation skills are really important in Real Life. So Pen is sometimes made to speak, and fear drives her, and she hears her voice, fast and low and uncertain, not her real voice at all, not how she sounds in her head, not how she sounds when she makes her friends in Latin class smile, not better, not more efficient, just faster.

The display says 1 MIN, which is two minutes since it said 3 MINS, so maybe things could go how they were meant to even without fear. In Lauren's house. That's all she needs to think and then she has an image of the house and her walking up to it, like she sees herself from outside, which is impossible, though they had filmed parts of it, so she had seen herself. After. The school hadn't taken it seriously enough, Sandy said. But that is also a bad thought, and she hears the woman-therapist's voice. 'Redirect, Pen.'

37

The boat-masts poke up over the wall, wrapped up for winter, though there are still people out sailing every week-end. The mirrored cladding of the lighthouse headquarters stares solidly back at her, she'll look at it for the one minute left. Irish Lights. People work in there, the guide had said on the public tour, to maintain the lights and beacons in fogs and storms and darkness. There are no lighthouse keepers any more, it seems, not in the way there was in the story she'd had as a child. Pen's mother had gone off script and invented adventures for Mrs Lighthouse Keeper, even though it wasn't written in the book, and Pen had cried and when Claire asked her why, she'd said, 'No, read the words that are there,' and her mother had said, 'What did I do to end up with such a literal child?'

To be in a lighthouse would mean constant fear, Pen thinks, would mean being responsible for the light crossing the waves, the weight of all those hulls, all those lives laying on you. She couldn't have been a lighthouse keeper. It was all electronic now, programmed, but still it would be a burden, to make the programme work, so that your body might not be in the lighthouse, no, it would be sitting at a desk pushing buttons, but your mind, all the time your mind would be balanced out on a rock in the wide water.

In Lauren's house. The girls had been sitting on Lauren's bed, with their backs against the wall, and Pen felt like she was auditioning. 'We'll only let you hang out with us if you do something,' they said. She nodded, and wished she had not come. She could hear Lauren's dad watching TV downstairs. 'Why did you do it?' Claire had asked afterwards, then said, too quickly, 'It's okay, it's not your fault.'

The train must be due, but the display screen has gone

blank. It's like there's no train any more, or a train to nowhere perhaps. This is the problem with signs, people look to them for instructions but if they disappear, then everyone feels lost. Pen knows the blankness only means the train is nearly here. The timetable was clear: 10:33. 'Don't overthink it,' people often say to Pen and then look smug. But most people actually under-think things, like not checking the timetable. Like that woman over there, tapping on her phone, is she afraid that 'I MIN' was just a fiction?

'First of all, you have to give us your phone,' Sarah said. 'It's against the rules of the club to communicate with outside parties.' Her face looked like a serious face. Sarah held out her hand and Pen didn't want to but she took her phone out and gave it to Sarah.

'Okay, freak, you can hang out with us if you get in the wardrobe,' Sarah said then and Chloe was saying, 'You know, maybe we should just leave it,' but the others said, 'No-o,' and laughed. Lauren got up silently and held the wardrobe door open. There were clothes on hangers and shoes and stuff and the rail didn't look very high. It was like they were all still for a second, just looking at the inside of the wardrobe. It looked small. Pen could have said, I won't fit in there, but she wanted them to like her.

So she got in. And Lauren closed the door.

And then it was silent.

Pen sees the train light appear at the end of the tunnel, and for this second, it is both due and here, transporting them all from fiction to reality, and the synchronicity of that is strangely satisfying. As the train passes her, perhaps Pen imagines it, but the driver looks like he's smiling at her. Why not, she thinks, allow herself to believe it? And when the train stops moving, it turns out that Pen is standing in the perfect place. The doors of the first carriage open when she pushes the button, and she looks for a seat, and there is one by the window and once she's sitting, and before the doors close and the train starts again, she opens her phone, and types: ON WAY! and presses send.

9.52 am

From her office window Ruth looks across at the grey arch-
ways. The building opposite had once been a bakery, which
can surprise her still, no trace of that now in the shops below,
blinds and musical instruments. 'One to conceal, one to
reveal,' Aidan had joked when they'd viewed the place first,
and she had laughed. Though maybe music was a mask, like
any other. Some clients ask Ruth if she knows this or that
song and ask her to listen, because it expresses their feelings,
because the singer's words convey them better than they can.
She'll listen, and then ask them to read the lyrics in their own
voices. It helps them to release something. Though Ruth fears
the opposite for them too, that to speak a secret can be a kind
of loss.

Anyway, playing an instrument is maybe more of a shield
than a mask. A violin at the chest, a guitar at the stomach,
turning one's back entirely at a piano. You were always liked
if you could play an instrument, you were called on at parties,
you were given space and brought close, all at the same time.
Aidan is right, Ruth has never figured that out, a way to be
easy around others. Perhaps it's her job that intimidates, the
idea that she might force a confession. 'You're not at work,'
Aidan reminds her before dinner parties.

Her job. Aidan was right there too, Ruth had thrown
herself into work. But it wasn't just because of the last few

years. She had always dreamed of an independent practice, the promise of making something for herself, surely he knew that? She and Lisa had talked about it since graduating, best friends and now business partners. Of course, it was Ruth who had led – drawing up plans, setting up meetings, finding the office. It was Ruth who had said to Lisa, 'Let's sign, let's just do it.' It was Ruth's idea to offer the first session for free. It was Ruth who had made it a success. No one can blame her for feeling proud. Ruth sighs, looks again at the building across from her. Somewhere behind the former bakery there was once an abbey. St Mary's. The estate agent had told her this, and Ruth had liked being let in on this history.

A man comes out of the music shop, carrying some kind of folded metal yoke, what is it, a music stand, maybe? Steps to the side, avoiding the woman on the phone who's pacing the pavement, pacing and chatting and waving her free hand. Ruth guesses she is speaking to a lover. Ruth looks again at the building opposite and wonders why the thing that is lost always seems more interesting. Perhaps the abbey was not attractive, was not wanted or useful or whatever buildings do for people.

In her twenties she had not thought she was creating a pattern, but it somehow was, and it kept on for over a decade. Time after time, man after man, there was always an ex-girlfriend or a big work project or an 'I'm just not looking for a relationship' until she could have screamed because what were they looking for? But the answer was frustratingly obvious. They had time to waste. So she'd stopped looking. And then, just like that, she'd found Aidan.

They had met years before, in college, so it wasn't like meeting for the first time. He had been first-year psychology too, but he'd transferred out in the second term. It was all Ruth could do to resurrect an image of him, to correlate it to this man in his thirties standing before her at Lisa's housewarming.

'I'm getting ahead in advertising,' he said.

Ruth smiled.

Aidan smiled.

And somehow that was it, she'd felt – yes, this is the person. Ridiculous, really. They had talked and laughed, and it was all going so well. But a gaggle of new people had arrived, and Aidan had drifted away. Trying to be subtle, Ruth had followed him when he next went to the kitchen, waving her empty wine glass, pretending surprise that he was going for a top-up too. And then they had sat on the stairs, just the two of them. It was while Ruth was telling some holiday anecdote that Aidan had reached across and taken her hand. It seemed audacious, that he could simply take her hand.

From that one gesture, they had become a pair. How Ruth had hated other people saying 'we', then suddenly she was doing it too. Looking at Aidan, with the pride of ownership. She loved the way his skin smelled. She loved that she came in bed with him without worrying what her face was doing. She loved that they wanted the same kind of life.

It's cold by the window. Ruth wishes she could override the landlord and put in double glazing. There are other things she would change in the room too, the door into the kitchen always jamming. She resents it suddenly, this place that has been her pride and her retreat. Look at me, doing it on my own, and she had made herself known, some articles, some phone-ins. But it's not enough.

Only a few minutes of peace left, and she should pull

herself together. She had run onto the bus, earlier, to get away from Stephen. What had he seen in her face, the fear maybe, the lines of worry? She should have asked him if he thought she was difficult. But you can't ambush people like that. Can't say, 'What's wrong with me?' And you really can't say, 'Why didn't you want me?'

'Men are for decoration,' her mother had said throughout her growing up. Intoning it as a lesson, as if admitting you needed a man – or any other person, really – was a kind of defeat. Ruth is not her mother, oh no, she's almost nauseous at the thought. But perhaps she is her creation, after all, perhaps that's why she's unable after all these years to do the basic things, like tell someone she needs them.

Almost ten o'clock. Ruth looks, yes, there's someone below, looking at the name plates. She sighs as she moves away from the window because this might be a long hour. It's always trickier with a new client, till you figure them out. All those expectations to negotiate.

The door chime goes.

Ruth presses the buzzer, hears the street door bang, and then feet on the stairs. Clearly a two-steps-at-a-time woman. Okay, then. Summon the calm face, the blank canvas, the friendly manner that says to this person they are welcome, that they have all your attention, that they're the first and only one.

Alice checks the time, then pauses for a moment, slips her phone in her pocket, touches the black paint of the front door. She wants to lean her head against it or maybe just go back inside. Perhaps she won't go, perhaps she'll say that she went, that she couldn't find Pen, that she had to come home. Then she could just spend the day watching TV. Maybe she could bring her duvet from her bed, make a nest. What would Mom say when she got home, something about 'Lady Muck'? Totally not worth it, the lecture and the *face of doom*. She could hide in her room, like, wouldn't it be perfect if you could do that thing with your mind where you stay in one place but you travel *mentally* into town and be there without being there. But then Pen would be left waiting. Alice imagines the way her shoulders would hunch and, okay, that makes Alice start moving. Already Pen has sent a load of texts, bing trill bing. And then there are the others wondering why Alice isn't in school, like the fake ones, HOPE YOU'RE OKAY, and the others, all, OOOH WHO'S GOT A HOT DATE and aubergine emojis. Everyone thinks they know Alice.

It's not exactly far to the station. Alice only has to walk to the end of the road, up to the lights, across the junction and the bit of Fairview Park, and then there it is, it's not a long commute at all. Her parents say this at least once a week in case they are meant to feel guilty for sending their daughter to school on the other side of the city. 'No one would say anything if you were only getting the bus,' Alice's mom says, but Alice has never said anything about the commute, it's all in her parents' heads. But then apparently she's not meant to say things like that either. 'No back chat, young lady,' or, 'I wasn't aware you studied philosophy at that school.' Shut up, basically.

At the end of the road, past the really nice greengrocer's, which was important because you should shop local, even though he sold beans from, like, Kenya, just past that shop there is a lamp post with a poster. It's been up for a while and Alice keeps expecting it to get torn down or to hear something said about it, but it's like no one else can see it, though lots of people must see it because it's got this massive Catholic logo and it's hung deliberately where all the people driving cars will glance at it on their way past to Clontarf or Howth or whatever.

LET KIDS BE KIDS

Yeah, whatever, Alice thinks, shrugging her shoulders. Except that's not how she really feels inside. Inside is all, 'Let me be what?' or even just, 'Let me be?' It's like the parable of the talents. 'Isn't it mean,' she'd asked Miss Taylor, 'to punish someone for minding their talent?' – which was what God had done to the guy who'd buried his bag of money. Miss Taylor had only smiled and said something about 'growing is caring'. Which was a shit answer. Alice's pocket buzzes.

On way! The message from Pen vibrates in Alice's hand.

Alice sees it and pauses, standing totally still on the street. Why is her stomach making her feel like she does before an exam? Maybe it would be easier, after all, just to turn around?

'I'm not going to talk about my childhood and stuff.'

Ciara is – what? – thirty-four. She'd stood for a while, unable or unwilling to take the offered chair, as if looking around for another option. She'd answered Ruth's opening questions with vague monosyllables, but at least she's actually sitting down now. Though she still seems determined not to engage.

'Perhaps we could move on from the basics. Can you tell me a little more about why you're here – what you'd like to get out of this?' Ruth says.

'Like I said, it's stress, there's so much stress, work–life balance, you know.' Ciara's voice hovers between anguish and boredom.

'So you want to deal with work stress?'

'I just want some tips, yeah, to deal with it, because I have this really important deadline and—' Ciara breaks off as her phone buzzes. She takes it out, checks it, pauses, then puts it on the table.

'I ask clients to switch phones off. They're quite distracting.' Ciara leaves the phone where it is. Ruth tries again. 'Prioritising yourself often means having boundaries.' Does Ciara shrug slightly? 'For work–life balance.'

'Yeah?' Ciara looks at Ruth, then slides the phone into her bag.

'Could you tell me a bit about the stress you're under. Do you work full-time?'

'Yeah. Yeah, I work in this big accounting firm.'

'So you're an accountant?'

'More management. See, my boss is on parental leave, which is great and all, 'cause I get a chance to do their job for the year and, my company, it's impossible to move up.'

'So it's a promotion?'

'Yeah, but even before it started, I got this thing where I just feel this nausea all the time. My boyfriend was all lovey-dovey and thinking, you know, baby, but it's not, course I know that. It's work stuff. Like I wake up in the night. I feel this – wave – of hating myself. I'm normally confident, yeah?'

'That must feel scary. Not to feel like yourself.'

'Yeah.'

'Is there one thing that's causing this stress, or is it the new job in general?'

'I have to organise this big end-of-year conference and it's just,' Ciara sighs deeply, 'the last thing I want to do.'

'When this nausea comes, can you tell me a little more about what that feels like?' Ruth asks.

'It's like nausea or like my whole body is trembling. Like my whole body is covered in goosebumps, even though I'm not cold. I keep wanting to cry. Or to just not, like, go into work. Pull a sickie. And all I keep thinking is, if I blow this, that's it – and that makes it worse.'

'What makes you think you'll blow it?'

'I told you, I'm not sleeping, feeling shit, my boyfriend says it's a lot of pressure.'

'Do you feel it's a lot of pressure?'

'And I just, like, I have to be the best at it all, like, better than the others, the boys, you know.' Ciara looks directly at Ruth.

'That does sound like a lot of pressure. Can I ask you how you imagine yourself at work, Ciara? For example, in your previous role, would you say you were the best?' Ruth asks.

'I'm,' Ciara looks surprised, 'I'm, yeah, I'm good at what I do.' A little confidence seeps into her body, stilling it.

'Perhaps you could tell me a little more about what you do?'

Ciara settles back a bit, her hands start to gesture. Ruth listens as she describes the office and the team and the different roles, 'the annual sales conference', and the office politics. The boyfriend slips in and out of the story as Ciara weaves a picture of a life that is balanced between work and home, different kinds of wants. This chat is good, Ruth feels, like a tiny holiday from the fact that they will have to circle back to the nausea and the sleeplessness.

'I keep feeling like everyone's waiting for me to fail. And I know it's terrible because if I let the thought, like, take over then I will. Fail.'

'I understand why you would feel sick about that. Can you tell me what you mean by "fail"?'

'I don't know.'

'Okay,' Ruth slows her pace, 'is there another way of saying "fail"?'

'Like, maybe I'm not good enough?'

'Do you think you're not good enough?'

'I don't know.' Ciara pauses. 'I keep clicking "unread" on my emails, 'cause I just don't have the energy to reply, you know?' She pauses again, hands opening towards Ruth in appeal. 'Maybe it would be easier to just jack it all in?'

'What makes you feel it would be easier?' Ruth asks, trying to make her voice sound gentle.

'There's this thing, some days, when I feel my skin, my actual skin, and it's like I'm one of those water balloons and if anything sharp comes near me, my skin will burst, it'll all flood out.'

'Have you said that to anyone before?'

Ciara nods.

'To someone at work?'

'No.' Her voice is a whisper. 'No, I told my boyfriend.'

'And how did it feel to share that with him?'

'He said I had to get checked out. Like, it wasn't normal.' Ciara stares at the table.

'How do you feel about that?'

Ciara shrugs.

'These sound like powerful emotions you're trying to contain.' And Ciara nods. 'Do you have anyone at work you can talk to? Anyone who could help?'

'This one person offered,' Ciara smiles grimly, 'but I was all "I got this" even though I blatantly don't got this at all.'

'I wonder,' Ruth risks, 'if there are any ways you might step back from the conference? It sounds like it's a lot. How would it feel if you didn't have to do it?'

'Fucking brilliant. But that's not going to happen.'

'Perhaps you could say to your line manager that you'd rather concentrate on other aspects of the work?' But it is the wrong question, the wrong moment.

'So you think I *am* fucking up?' and suddenly the calm of the last twenty minutes is gone. 'I don't want people to laugh at me. I just want,' Ciara leans forward, 'I just want something to help me sleep. If I could sleep, if I could sleep, I'd be fine.

My boyfriend off my back. My work. I could go back to being me. Seriously, can't you prescribe me something?'

Ruth pauses, then says, 'We could discuss a GP referral letter.' Another pause as Ciara stares at her. 'And I'm not ruling it out, but I don't think sleeping pills are going to—'

'To be honest, I don't think this is working.' Ciara is suddenly on her feet, bag over her shoulder. 'Aren't you meant to be giving me something, helping me?'

10.33 am

If you face backwards, the world doesn't come at you. Pen sees the bay instead, then high walls before more sea at Blackrock, walls to protect the railway or the public? Both. Her mother talks about checking the tides because her ambition is to walk from Seapoint to Sandymount, but someone had said it couldn't be done, that there was a stream at Blackrock. Claire says that she's sceptical about that, but Pen doesn't think she's looked up the tides or made a plan to actually do it. Pen thinks of it as a file in her mum's brain, making that flashing clicking noise, and sometimes she wants to ask her if it ever gets too much for her too.

Is it better to have unfulfilled ambitions or to have fewer plans that you actually carry out? Which makes you feel smaller? Is Pen a small person? 'Everyone struggles,' the woman-therapist said at the start. 'Everyone is carrying something.' Then the woman-therapist said that lots of people try to hide the thing they're carrying, so that even for people without sensory processing differences, emotions can be really hard to read. Basically, thinks Pen, the entire rom-com genre is proof that feelings aren't easy.

Pen looks at the people on the train. They are staring out the window or at their phones. One man is shaking a newspaper. Pen studies the green blur of the grass outside going by which is weird to look at because it keeps disappearing but also easier to look at than people. She wonders what 'something' the man with the newspaper has or the woman with the buggy, what are they carrying? Pen imagines them, shouldering their sadness and worry and fear like grey backpacks. There were yellow and orange backpacks too for the happy people, but even they, it stood to reason, had something to be sad about. Even Lauren, maybe. That was the point, you only saw parts of people. You could skip faces and just concentrate on these, the bags they carry, and maybe that way you could understand the important things about a person. How they were impatient, or sad, or angry, or ignored you. Or were mean.

The salt marsh, even though it is brown and briny and smells in summer, is one of Pen's favourite places. Her sister always says she thinks it's ugly, wrinkling up her nose, but Pen likes it for that reason. Three things about the salt marsh: one, it survives despite its swampy appearance; two, it's cool because nature shouldn't always have to be pretty; three, it is a sanctuary (*sanctus* meaning holy). Pen read an article last year which said that although people are only 0.001 per cent of all life on earth, they've killed most of the other types of mammals. It's called species loneliness.

If you are vulnerable, then you need protection. This makes sense to Pen, but her dad says that everyone just needs to toughen up. Grit, that's what he thinks they all need. Pen thinks she could write a handbook about grit or that other thing, resilience, and that in this handbook she would explain that these words only exist to make other people feel bigger. But she doesn't say this back to him. She doesn't say that what people call resilience is actually just a shell you build so that no one can see you on the inside. She doesn't say that resilience is an excuse, for people who don't want to actually do the thing that would help you not-be-vulnerable. She doesn't say that grit is actually an idea to make other people feel better for sending you out into the world to get hurt, over and over. None of this is said because if you said it then you were not being resilient.

Sometimes it is the absence of resilience that makes things beautiful. Sometimes being 'thin-skinned' means you can feel the beautiful things more. The low sunlight in the winter. The sound of Alice's voice. *Papiliones*. Do butterflies like the salt marsh? It's famous for the birds, and each time Pen is on the train she thinks she will learn all the names of all the birds. She only knows enough to tell Soraya the lagoon is of ornithological importance, at which Soraya rolls her eyes, which is basically like watching an emoji. Pen will get a bird book from the library, zero carbon. They all already travel by public transport as much as possible, that puts them ahead, that says they are officially good people. Labelling things good or bad is not one of the strategies recommended by Pen's woman-therapist – she says, 'Sustaining or draining?' and that things aren't good or bad because they're actually neutral, it's-how-you-feel-about-them. But Pen prefers her way, even if sometimes it's hard to decide.

Pen hopes she gets to the station first, she likes to wait, to be ready, to be not rushing, to look around. But she also doesn't want to wait too long, that makes her nervous. There are two ticks so Alice has read the message, is she on her way too? Alice only has three stops into town so maybe she's at the station or walking there. Sydney Parade is the next stop, but who was Sydney? They learn stuff in school (she should be in school!) but Pen reckons there is more that they don't learn, like how to be and what the world really means.

Sandy wants her to be a doctor or an architect, she's only

okay at maths though. Mostly she likes the way numbers measure things and how they have rules, like pi (π) is interesting, because most people think of it as just 3.14 but actually it's 3.14159265 and that's just the beginning, you could go on, because it's an irrational real number. Pen can think about things like that for ages, about how you can only really understand things if you include all the details even if all the details are, basically, inconvenient because no one has the time to do all the decimal places of pi. But Pen isn't one of those maths geniuses like in all the films about people with brains like hers, as if you can't be autistic and average at the same time, you have to be gifted to be interesting. Pen likes the idea of designing things, but the buildings she described to her dad made him laugh. 'Buildings are meant for people, Pen,' he said, and her vision of empty white rooms dissolved. Even if you know maths really well, even if you know all the numbers that make up every single thing, it will never make up for not knowing people.

When she'd read that book by Virginia Woolf last summer, about the man with shell shock, Pen had understood why he had jumped from the window, and she had also understood how hard it was for his wife, who could not help him. So now Pen thinks she might study English. She likes how reading gives you time to think, that emotions don't change if they're written down. Sometimes Pen thinks her mother wants her to be more like her, she reads poetry to her and Soraya, takes Pen to plays, telling her stories of being pregnant and doing her PhD at the same time, as if by osmosis Pen absorbed her love for words, as if they have this bond. But Pen suspects Claire sees words as ways to join the world, and not, like Pen does, as a kind of space. Pen doesn't say this, though, because her mum tries really hard. But sometimes there are these jolts of disconnection, like when they go on family outings and she watches her sister and mother laugh together, or when Claire says, 'Thank you for coming with us,' as if Pen is not part of this family, as if she will always be an outsider.

Pen's mother is a warrior. Which somehow feels sustaining and draining all at the same time, but she can't say that either because other people are always telling Pen how lucky she is to have her mum. 'She didn't give up,' they say. It's maybe the one thing her parents agree on. Resilience.

Pen's phone buzzes. She grins.

ON WAY TOO! ♡

10.38 am

Standing by the water is a bit cold, but the view is worth it, or that's what Aidan tells himself. There are rowers on the Thames, and he is surprised they are still allowed, what with the water taxis and barges chugging past the South Bank. Perhaps he'll stay and look at this view, get a coffee at one of the container thingies? But no, that's for tourists, and besides, it's not warm enough, perhaps there's somewhere more sheltered, further on. Undecided, he watches the rowers until they are out of sight, under the bridge. Vague strands of noise float over the water, and Aidan turns to see a small stream of people hurrying towards Westminster, festooned with funereal banners, yelling already.

WHAT DO WE WANT? CLIMATE JUSTICE!
WHEN DO WE WANT IT? BEFORE IT'S TOO LATE!

He envies them their faith. Aidan starts to walk, weaving between the stragglers, past the concrete theatre. They'd been to a matinee show there once, several hours of American melodrama. On the way in, Ruth had pulled a face, and said she was squelching, her boots must have let in rain as they'd walked. 'Take them off,' he'd said as soon as they were sitting, 'or you'll get pneumonia.' Then he'd disappeared, making it back just as the ushers were closing the doors. 'Here,' and he gave Ruth a pair of novelty socks from the gift shop. 'My hero,' Ruth had whispered. Aidan glances up at the posters for Gabriel's Wharf, decides not to get coffee after all. Do you think, he'd wanted to ask her last night, do you think those people are gone?

The Oxo Tower looms up, he goes in under its arches, narrower here along the water. A group of kids pass him out, skateboards under their arms. He's under Blackfriars now, with its tiled mural. Slow down, Aidan, no need to race. Already, the awkward bulk of Tate Modern is ahead. In theory, he's on his way to see a show, 'In Real Life'. Ruth had sent him a link to the exhibition, said something about the artist's use of colour, and he'd even mentioned it to her last night, another one of his justifications. Now he's here, though, he can't face it. He has too much real life, he thinks, but Christ, what a crank that makes him sound. 'I like it,' Ruth would always say, lingering by a picture he had zoomed past, 'I like it.' The confidence it takes just to know what you like, to declare it like a fact. He goes on. Past the wobbly bridge, St Paul's across the water. Pause to look, while a couple of joggers pump by. Aidan is meant to be deciding how to leave his wife, but everywhere he looks, he sees signs of her.

Back when they'd started, it had been him pursuing her. 'Oh, you're dating the fortress,' his friend Paul had said, and Aidan had smiled and nodded, silently thinking, ah, just you watch, I'll make her mine. But after their first night together, he'd realised this resolution wasn't without risk. Instead of sleepily re-enacting last night's fun, Aidan found himself pulling on running shorts and trainers, borrowed from her housemate

('Yeah, no problem, pal'), trying to ignore his morning-after hangover. Standing up, a bit dizzy, he realised Ruth was already ahead of him, car keys in hand. Aidan paused at the door.

'It's freezing!'

'It's not, anyway you'll get used to it,' Ruth said, 'and you can warm up in the car.'

'We could just go back to bed?' The request was meant to come out as romantic, but it sounded wheedling. Ruth gave him a look. 'Or we could go for a run!' His reward, a smile.

In the park, Ruth did a few stretches while Aidan half-heartedly jumped up and down on the spot. His claim that he loved exercise, *loved it*, was getting more dubious by the second.

'Once around the course?' Ruth asked.

Within a few minutes, Aidan was seriously out of breath. 'I think I'm getting a stitch.' Heart attack more likely.

'You'll run easier if you lift your chin.'

Aidan complied, but it made him feel dizzier, the sky tilting in and out of view.

'Imagine you have a rod from the top of your head,' Ruth said, 'going all the way down to your feet, through your shoulders, hips, knees and ankles, all in a straight line.'

How was she managing to talk and run at the same time? A rod? Aidan tried to imagine it, but it only made his whole body feel even stiffer. Christ, he could barely lift his legs. And since when was Ruth an expert on bodies? Counselling she'd said, and he'd imagined a quiet, sensitive type.

'Chin up!'

It was all he could do not to tell her to fuck off. But soon he could see the gate, the end of the course. He'd made it. 'It's been a while,' he panted, barely upright, expecting her to jeer.

'Me too,' she said. 'I'm bright red!'

Ruth leaned in then to kiss him, a sweaty kiss, and she was, he hadn't even noticed, she was red in the face and out of breath too.

'We went running,' Ruth said, 'together!'

In the car it was back to the instructions, but Aidan found the coaching easier to take somehow.

'Exhale as far as you can,' Ruth said.

He obediently blew the air out as far as he could.

'Now see if you can squeeze any more out.'

And surprisingly, Aidan could breathe out even more, it was as if he could feel the bottom of his lungs contract.

'It's called grey air, they taught me it in yoga, we carry all this stale air around with us.'

Back at her place, Aidan had taken charge of breakfast: toast, eggs, the works.

'I could get used to this,' Ruth said, marvelling at the spread.

'I like that idea,' Aidan said. 'Like happily domesticating animals.' They both laughed and in that second, Aidan thought, I love you.

It's Aidan, of course, who still runs (though only occasionally), Ruth who gave it up. Aidan pauses again, leaning against a railing. Christ, it really doesn't help to remember the good parts. Look at the river, distract yourself with that. This must be Bankside, it's a bit anonymous. Is the building across the river some kind of government department, it looks it, but then it's hard to know in London.

What was it Ruth had said last night – 'Do you want easy?' He could have screamed, because hadn't he been through the same things as her? Didn't they both want – deserve – some kind of ease? Aidan pulls his scarf a little closer, walks on.

11.10 am

After the train stops you have to wait a few seconds for the doors to release. The button lights up green and Pen enjoys pushing it, she's not a kid but it's still good. Her travel card beeps at the gates and she manages not to freak out at the person coming through too closely behind her, she just breathes, takes the escalator handrail, and thinks of the colour blue. You can't own a colour, but you can hold it so it's always there, you can always find something blue to look at, especially the sky (today the sky is grey, but there is blue behind the cloud). The box around the screen listing all the trains is a dark blue, focus on that. When Pen said that blue makes her feel most herself (sustaining), Sandy said 'that's emotion' with a high note in his voice.

Pen is here before Alice, which is good, she can stand with a view of the southbound stairs, by the key-cutting place opposite the doughnut shop. Maybe she should buy Alice a doughnut? Good or bad idea? Not good for you, but then that's what makes it a treat. Pen should avoid spikes in blood sugar because they make her very good and then very bad. The sound of a train overhead. She'd rather be here waiting, especially what if she chose the wrong flavour, she'd have to make a quick decision, which is not her least-favourite-thing but not good either. Pen may as well save her strength for all the ways she will have to be not-like-herself today.

There is a stream of people hurrying past now and if Pen is reading them right, they all have worried faces, grey backpacks. 'Is life meaningful?' 'Does she love me?' 'Am I enough?' Pen asked Claire once what people think about and that was the list she gave, she hadn't even thought about it. But Claire had laughed then and said, actually, they were probably all thinking, 'Will it rain?' or, 'Am I late?' It wasn't ever as philosophical as you imagined. Pen had nodded and Claire had said, 'A penny for them,' which didn't make sense because they don't have pennies any more, they have cents, and besides, people don't give you any kind of money for saying what you think. But Pen had said this to Alice once, and she'd said, 'Except, like, in newspapers and on YouTube where you get lots of money for saying what you think,' which was a fair point. To her mother, Pen had said she wasn't thinking anything, which was not quite true, it was just better to keep some things to herself. For some reason this made Claire laugh again, and then she said Pen would never be judgemental because she never assumed she knew what people were.

The crowd is lessening so perhaps that wasn't Alice's train at all. Perhaps Alice isn't really coming, perhaps she doesn't know that this is a date, perhaps she is not looking forward to it the way Pen has been for so long?

But here is Alice. (*Ecce! In pictura!*) Pen sees the top of a reddish fair head, and it's definitely her, she'd know her anywhere. Anywhere. Pen feels her inside light up as they shimmy hands at each other, Alice holding hers up, above her head, still halfway across the ticket hall, so Pen gets to enjoy her for longer and this is what she likes so much – that Alice literally does not care what anyone else thinks.

'Wow, we're really doing this, Pen! I'm so excited. But also nervous too, you know what I mean?'

Alice is perfect. Alice is a wave of perfect. Maybe that's why Pen is having difficulty finding her breath. Smile, she tells her face, not wanting to lose the moment that they're standing here together, the beginning of the day which is a date, though Alice maybe doesn't know that yet. Alice's eyes squash together, Pen is definitely smiling now, this is what other people do, every day, without even thinking.

'Do you want to go?'

'Yeah! Do you think,' Alice asks as they turn left out the door, 'there will be many people there already?'

Two girls leave the railway station, walking closely together, along a pavement not crowded, the sky brightening as they move southwards, pausing at the junction, crossing to the island then to the pavement, round where the road opens out wider and they can see the trees. Two girls see the crash barriers under this bigger sky. They pause, suddenly uncertain. Was it here they were to be? Was it today, not elsewhere, not another day? Two girls.

'Wow, the whole street is shut off,' Alice says.

'Wow,' says Pen.

'Look,' Alice points towards the top of the railed-in park, 'there's people up there.'

Two girls wait, cross when the lights change. Walk without saying anything, but excited, definitely excited. Important, even.

Pen sees people in bright yellow vests. On the backs they have symbols, a stylised hourglass, and too late she thinks she should have painted something to speak for her, maybe on an old T-shirt, or even on her mac.

'Hi, are you from Extinction Rebellion?' Alice's voice sounds high-pitched.

'Yeah, do you want to know about the protest?'

'Actually,' Pen clears her throat, 'is Jo around? We kind of know her.' Jo is Claire's student, she is their pass to be here, to be one of them.

'Em,' says the woman, 'do you know a Jo?' She's looking at the guy, they're looking at each other, shaking heads. 'No worries,' she shrugs. 'I'm Sinéad and this is David.'

'Hi,' he says, nodding.

'We're, em, gathering at half twelve at the Dáil,' Sinéad says. 'There'll be lots more people then, and we're walking at one. There's signs and leaflets,' she gestures behind her, 'over at the stand, that's only getting set up, but you can head over there?'

'Thanks, guys,' Alice says, 'cool, thanks.'

Alice looks embarrassed maybe, but Pen could float because she spoke to a stranger.

Two girls move together and it's a few steps only to get to the stall. Where they stand and nod to the people doing the setting-up. Where they pause at the kerb. Sure. Unsure.

'Look,' Pen says, pointing to the signs stacked against the railings, ' "Rebel for Life".'

'Yeah, and "The Oceans are Rising B U T S O A R E W E". Cool,' Alice nods, smiling.

Two girls hover on the edge, watching the people assembling metal poles for the stalls. If they just stand here, will someone notice them?

'I don't see anyone else as young as us,' Pen whispers.

'But that's why it's so much cooler,' Alice whispers back, 'not just the people from school, not just kids being, like, indulged.'

Pen nods, but she needs something to do. Something to do or a destination. Standing here is too aimless, she'll begin counting soon, not people because they move around too much, but the railings, the front doors, the colour blue, things to give the world solidity. She looks at Alice, and her face seems blank too.

Two girls on the south side of Merrion Square. Surrounded by buildings so tall, can people even still live in them? They've been here before, of course they have, to the Dead Zoo with their parents. But that was then. Now is different, they're different, the situation is different. Urgent. They look around them. Slate-grey sky. Slate-grey ground. Trees whispering.

Limbo again.

Shy again.

No blue.

'Are you looking to help?' an older man says, coming over to them with a stack of leaflets. And when they nod, both temporarily muted, he says, 'Okay, take some of these, hand them out over there, catch some of the foot traffic.' His arm waves towards where they've come from.

'Yeah, great,' Alice says.

Pen nods and Alice divides the leaflets.

Two girls walk with purpose, saving the planet, saved for a while themselves.

11.30 am

She always feels like shit after a client leaves like that. People have to unravel themselves and Ruth facilitates, oh, as much as she can. But what can you do for a client who does not, actually, want to? As she pushes notes into the buff folder, Ruth wonders if Ciara had thought she was a man, she only has her initial, 'Dr R. Ryan', on the list. But gender wasn't the problem: Ruth just wasn't sympathetic enough. On another day she would have handled the session better. She won't be surprised if Ciara does not come back.

Ruth watches a strand of old spiderweb waving gently in the ceiling corner and wonders where the breeze is coming from. Those windows. It can't be easy to own a building like this, Ruth reminds herself each time the floor creaks or the walls have that almost-damp coldness. Perhaps she and Lisa should try to buy or get a longer lease somewhere else. But the rents! The windows weren't so bad.

Anthony had asked about their extension and Ruth thinks of it now, how she and Aidan had gone to practically every showroom in the city, trying to decide on fixtures and fittings, weighing up each choice as if this one – double or triple glazing, wood or laminate – would determine the happiness of their lives to come. When they had first bought the house, of course, they'd inherited the last owner's tastes and decisions. As that first year rolled into winter Ruth had tried to change the programming for the heating. Fiddly and annoying, the controls were wedged in under the stairs, and Ruth should have asked Aidan to do it, really, he was more patient. She cursed as the dial stuck and the little plastic teeth would not release their bite. She had pushed it harder and heard a snapping sound, her heart sank, Aidan would blame her. But later when she'd told him, he had only made a rueful face, said it was just for a few more months, till they could afford a new boiler, a new system. 'Let me have a look,' he'd said, and they had both crammed their heads into the narrow space, Ruth holding the torch, illuminating the row of broken tines. 'Ah,' he'd said, and twisted the dial 180 degrees. It was an obvious fix, just change the dial by twelve hours, the system wouldn't know the difference. 'Genius,' Ruth said, and Aidan turned with a grin, almost bashing his head on the door lintel as they pulled out. 'We're time travellers, living in the future,' he said, and Ruth had laughed. It must be six, seven years ago, now? The sudden grief surprises her and Ruth thinks that maybe it does not help to remember the good bits.

'Why is that the hardest thing for you to say?' he had asked recently, some dig about her not asking for help. The hardest thing. Even after all these years of practice she could not determine, with precision, what was the hardest thing for people to admit. It was to do with shame, usually. 'Do you hear yourself?' Ruth wanted to ask him back, because his tone had been so cold, it was hard to believe someone who loved you could speak to you that way. It was like one of her lecturers had said about addiction, the turning point is always earlier than you think.

'Look, babe, the clinic is offering free tests, it's like a sign,' Ruth said, pointing at the screen, the floating image of the doctor in a white coat, the clinic banner, the smiling nurse. ' "Book a free AMH test to check your ovarian reserve",' she read. 'It's a perk of "fertility awareness week", apparently.' Ruth smiled because this was her idea, they had the house, spare bedrooms, the wedding a month away, surely they wanted the same thing? She smiled at Aidan, because she had wanted it for so long, this idea of a baby, that it was as if the baby were real, just waiting to be pulled into being, to be loved.

Ruth shouldn't have pushed Ciara, it was far too soon. She normally has more margin, today everything seems on edge. Hard to admit that what provoked her most was Ciara's youth. All her options. Someone is shouting on the street outside, something about, 'Open the . . . can't you, Jimmy.' It's no good. Ruth can't concentrate enough to do these notes, she cannot think of a single question to ask either Anthony or Ciara (if she even comes again) that would open up their lives. She shivers and thinks that they should get one of those oil-filled radiators, for the winter. Ruth taps on the keyboard and the screen flashes into life.

'Jimmy,' the voice from the street cries, plaintive now.

The walkway past the Globe is narrower than he'd remembered. When Aidan had set out, he thought he'd get food somewhere in Borough Market. But as he reaches the side entrance, the stalls and the options and the idea of making a choice are overwhelming. He doesn't even register it as a decision, just keeps going. Past a vacant lot, under a grimy train bridge, then along a shiny, oddly empty street. It's starting to rain a bit, though, and there's no café or even a shop. Perhaps he'll get a Tube back to the hotel, get his case, head to the airport early. But is there even a station near here? Ridiculous to be lost like this.

'Lots of people need help, Ruth,' he'd said. 'It doesn't mean there's anything wrong with us.' It had been Ruth who'd been so keen to get her eggs tested in the first place, a weird kind of wedding present, she'd said. But it hadn't been so celebratory when the results came back, and she hadn't even wanted to discuss it. 'We knew we'd have to start soon,' he'd said. 'Let's just see what the consultant has to say.' Even Aidan had to admit, though, that the waiting room was the opposite of what they'd both imagined lay ahead when he'd turned to Ruth and said, 'Let's be a family.'

There were two other couples sitting there, sharing the wrong kind of silence, risking covert looks at the thank-you cards and baby pictures on side tables and window ledges. He'd almost turned to her then, had almost said, 'Okay, you're right, let's go, let's get our baby the old-fashioned way.' But instead he'd fixed a half-smile on his face, and when the nurse had called their names, they'd got up and followed her, through another door, into an office they would come to know too well. They had taken their seats on one side of the desk, holding hands now, saying the things they'd rehearsed, listening to the explanations, to the acronyms and statistics. They'd kept nodding, like it was all so reasonable.

The first injection had taken them nearly half an hour to get in at all. Ruth on the bed, Aidan with the needle, angled the way the nurse had shown them. Terrified of hurting her. Did they really have to do this a hundred times? 'Maybe it will work on the first cycle,' Ruth had said, smiling the smile he loved. And the first treatment had produced twenty-eight follicles, which seemed like good news. But after triggering, only ten eggs were collected, and then only four had matured. And though all four fertilised, by day five only one embryo was suitable for transfer. Probably not on the first cycle, then, Aidan had realised. So, on day ten, when Ruth insisted on taking an early test, he had been surprised by her look of joy as two pink lines slowly emerged, surprised by his own sense of hope. She did another then, to make sure, a digital version this time, which three minutes later actually said 'PREGNANT' in its little window. After Ruth had left the room to call the clinic, Aidan had put the test down, counted to ten, picked it up and looked at it again. Still pregnant.

At the clinic, they were all so happy for them. But when the blood results came back, the doctor said the Beta hCG level was only 47. He explained that 50 was the minimum, and Aidan realised that 'PREGNANT' didn't really mean anything.

'It may go up, it's early days,' the doctor said, they should be hopeful, perhaps it was just a delayed implantation. They would do another blood test in a few days. And, in fact, after the weekend the levels had gone up a little. Ruth had kept taking the meds, he had kept giving the shots. A week later, the numbers had risen again, but still not like they were meant to. And a few days after that, Ruth had started a heavy period. Surprised by the scale of his grief, Aidan had said, 'We'll try again,' and been relieved when Ruth had nodded. He'd thanked her, and she'd said, 'Why are you thanking me, we're in this together.'

Aidan stands bereft, on a grey pavement in London, with no idea of why he is here and not at home, not with Ruth, not sharing any of this with her. It is all so sad, suddenly, the wasted day and the wasted life and . . . the waste. His breath catches in his chest. Breathe deeply, well, there was a limit to what that could cure, and he cannot, he has tried, he cannot find a way to release his grief this time. He wants to ask her, to ask his wife, to put it right. Fix me, he wants to say. Or release me.

The trouble with doing it on your own, Ruth thinks, is how alone you are. Sometimes it is as if there are no other bodies in this building, oh, a door closing to another room, or a floorboard squeaking somewhere, the click of a switch, or even the flush of the loo on the landing (another dispute with the landlord, because the cubicle is just too small, too exposed, there on the landing, for any comfort, material or personal). But the building is mostly quiet. The street can be heard, in waves, there are people out there, life happening. Perhaps she should go out. She's not due at the hospital until two (*only a check-up*). Or perhaps she'll just slump under her desk, curl into a ball, hope that the world will just go away. 'Do you know that way,' a teacher had asked her once, 'how sometimes you feel like you are in a film?' He had a habit, he confessed, of pretending while he was doing things, supermarket shopping or making dinner, that he was performing his life.

Ruth puts on her coat, the notes can wait, the windows can be left, she will go out and forget the way the room looks, both expectant and forlorn. The door softly thuds behind her, and the stairs are dark. She can't be bothered with the light, so she feels her way down, back through the narrow hall. She and Lisa had speculated about painting it, or hanging posters, but then it had been three years since they took the rooms, their shared practice, and it seemed to be going well, in fact, it took all their time, so the posters and the paint, the windows, all got forgotten. (Though the toilet, perhaps they could at least paint that when Lisa gets back from her leave.) Out on Capel Street the air is milder than earlier, Ruth loosens her scarf. Walking towards the river, she changes her mind, turns left.

Ruth wants so often to tell clients that they are normal, but that, she suspects, is not what they want to hear. For some it was a comfort, to know that how they felt or what they had done or had had done to them did not make them different, it made them the same. Their lives were not extraordinary. But for Ciara, as for Anthony, now she thinks about it, this sameness was not what they wanted.

The air is fresh, and this was a good idea, walking, moving, though it is hard to avoid, completely, the sense that she's running away. (*Run! Stay!*) Abbey Street is easier than the quays, less stressful than going through Temple Bar, though the street's quietness is not a good thing, on the whole. Strange that the city had changed so little since she was a kid. Apartments was the main thing. So many of them thrown up. Damp. Fire risk. Ahead there is a couple, or a pair of boys, close together, some kind of dispute, looking at something together, then an embrace. A barber's, always annoying how men's haircuts were cheaper, as if they had fewer hairs. Ruth steps into the road to avoid the group of boys, bikes on pavements, taking up all the space, the irony of the empty road, and she wonders what would happen if you did that, just walked into the road and stayed there, walked slowly so the traffic built up behind you, horns going and people yelling, and you, there, defiant, for once refusing to let another person's needs come first. 'No need to be a drama queen,' another of her mother's observations.

Ruth passes one of the city's many language schools, students clumped together, T-shirts in October. Ahead, she sees the lurid sign for the leprechaun museum and wonders if it's any good, if her godson would enjoy it? She should take him to more things, but Ruth is too aware of being a pretend aunt, and she can still feel the childhood tedium of being made to go to shows aimed at children that were slightly too young for her, the horror of being asked how she was getting on at school. She had taken him, Conor, to the Sea Life place at Bray one bank holiday and it had not been a huge success, he was either too small or not small enough, and the tanks were cramped, seemed cruel. The Zoo had been better, they had gone in a group for his birthday and had seen elephants, tigers, giraffes. She had bought him a stuffed animal in the shop, though she has no memory of what it was – toucan? tiger cub? She had loved it when he took her hand, she did it for those moments of love. *No – not that – think of something else.* How did leprechauns come about anyway? It was true, apparently, that Ireland had more rainbows, something to do with latitude, or the fact that it was always raining. Where the pot of gold came in she isn't sure, but she had passionately believed in it as a child, urging her mother to drive in pursuit of the rainbow's end. It's over there.

It's too early to cross the river, acres of time till her appointment. Ruth hates dawdling. She should have stayed at her desk, tried to come up with some new thoughts after all, to finish some paperwork, at least she could have done some emails (another kind of displacement), but she has not and so she stands on the pavement edge, undecided. A tram is leaving the stop and Ruth pauses to let the mill of people pass. There is a newspaper abandoned on the bench in the shelter.

TURKISH ASSAULT ON KURDISH FORCES. AN IMPEACH-
MENT. HOMELESSNESS.

Ruth looks up to see where the noise is coming from, notices
a blonde woman with a buggy, its cargo screaming. They're
close to her, manoeuvring onto the pavement, stopping by
her. 'Fuck's sake, shut the fuck up!' There is something about
that, the child, suddenly silent, that arrests Ruth. Too late, she
realises the mother has seen her staring. Ruth steps into the
road, without a glance for the traffic. A bike swerves. 'Sorry,'
she calls out, too late. Glancing back, Ruth sees the woman
bending over the child. What is she doing? Just giving the
little thing a bag of sweets, it looks like. There had been an
occasion when Ruth had spoken out. On the bus one evening, a man was letting a very young child swig from a bottle
of Calpol. Ruth had waited for a while, but the third time he
did it, she said, 'I don't think you should do that.' And she
had felt every person around her, their attention keen on her,
as the man had shouted, 'Mind your own business, cow!' Of
course, Ruth had let it go. She feels even now the mix of shame
and anger, thinks of the number of times she'd been hit or
screamed at in public, and no one had ever said anything, not
to her mother with her nice middle-class accent. And Ruth is
not sure why her mother is in her mind so much today, when
she can go weeks without a thought of her, for her, and it is
ironic, almost, when her mother was the last person she would
ever confide in.

Ruth rounds onto Liffey Street, and has to step into the
road again, the pavement full with a huddle of tourists and
a man on his phone. Walking is like an antidote to the counselling room, perhaps it is too intense this one-on-one all the
time. She has been considering a request for group sessions,

a support group for teenagers. She imagines them, a disconsolate circle, or maybe not, maybe they would be loud, full of life, which is even more terrifying.

Ruth doesn't offer family counselling. Finally, Ruth had said, in desperation, 'Well, Mum, maybe we should talk to someone, you know, together,' and her mother, to both their astonishment, had mutely nodded. But it had not been a success. They had met on the steps outside, sat next to each other in the waiting room, her mother's body jerking when their names were called. Ruth had hoped for – what? – a new beginning. She could no longer carry her mother's anger (she could not, she would not). But as she began to speak, it was something innocuous enough, an opening gambit, her mother's head had shot back as if she had been whipped. That, Ruth had wanted to say, that was *nothing*. Her mother's constant fury, that was what she'd wanted to tell the therapist about, to find an ally against. But the minutes had dragged by, with each of them answering every question only yes or no. At the end Ruth had apologised to the therapist as they left, nodding when he'd said perhaps they weren't ready yet and he was here if she wanted to come alone. What, though, Ruth suddenly wonders, what had her mother wanted to say?

Across the road had been a food court, there was an archway just there surely, leading through to stalls and cafés. Had it just vanished, Epicurean something it's called. Was called. Now just a giant discount store, the huge coffee chain opposite.

Ruth had wanted a daughter herself. She would do it all differently. She'd – *No* – *think of something else.*

The archway is totally gone, but you can still get kebabs at 'Istanbel's Hyderabad House', whoever named it covering all the bases. And there's still the health-food place, the chocolate café. But the trimmings shop opposite is gone, where she'd bought ribbons, bedecking herself, a teenager tying black lace around her neck. Ruth glances at her watch, still too early.

Peering down the quay, the bookshop is still there at least. Ruth's feet take her forward and halt before the window of the Winding Stair. The books are hanging, like a mobile, like they have escaped the prim confines of a bookcase, the orange covers of the classics mixed in with new books. She's relieved that paper is still a thing, the smell of a book, it's not the same reading on a screen. There are postcards and tote bags too. What was this one, 'My mistakes are my,' what, the bag was folded a bit, oh, 'my life.' Yes.

Ruth suddenly wants *this*. To do nothing with her days but read. A gentle kind of protest. (She will do the teenager thing, it will be a change.) But as her eyes skim over the books' surfaces, it feels too much. Perhaps she should buy one? But do I want to carry it all day? Ruth hovers at the window, slowly one cover coming into focus. She sees the drape of red fabric across the bodies, enfolding them, the tender embrace. A Schiele painting. She leans closer, reads the little Post-it blurb attached to the cover, 'Staff Pick . . . stories . . . women'. The handwriting is too small. She does not care, anyway, about the contents, it is the image. They had seen the show together, 'Modern Something' or '20th Century Something' or 'Ways of Something', the exhibition title eludes her, but the memory is strong. How they had stood before the picture, how they had been stilled by its tenderness, how Aidan had reached his hand for hers, fingers entwining. *Mother and Daughter*. It is their togetherness she remembers. Ruth's hand trembles now. It could not be gone, all of it, surely?

At the register, the bookseller rings it up. Ruth asks a

favour. 'Could I pick it up on my way back, I have a meeting and,' she shows her already-full bag, 'I'd rather not carry it around all day.'

The woman smiles. 'Of course, I'll keep it behind the counter, just ask for it. I'll put your name on the bag, Ruth Ryan, okay?' Ruth nods. 'Nice alliteration.'

It is a bookish thing to say.

And she is on the street again.

Through Merchant's Arch, up Crown Alley, which had seemed so exciting when you were fifteen and now, well, was it only for tourists? The building site ahead forces her to the left and around and on to College Green. She waits for the lights to change, crosses, and now here is Trinity Street and the pub on the corner, scene of so many student nights and, yes, the ATM still there across the road, the source of cash for one last drink. The street is for pedestrians now. The window of Avoca, brightly coloured blankets. Ruth had gone through a phase of buying them for friends' babies, she inherited one herself from a similar gift to her mother, 'This blanket is older than you,' said so many times. Blue mohair, a mauve stripe. But the shop is owned now by that company that sells terrible food to asylum centres, she hasn't been in since. ('What's the point of a boycott, if no one knows?' Aidan said.) Ruth turns right, perhaps she will walk up Grafton Street, eat somewhere near the Green? She passes Brown Thomas with all its expensive, shiny things – and feels sick, suddenly, at the idea of it all and turns and goes back down to Nassau Street.

There is a gap at the corner of Dawson Street where there used to be a building, one of those ugly seventies constructions, eighties maybe, and now there is sky where there had been brown brick. The way things can disappear amazes her, the vanished arch, now this, from solid to air. Through the gap she sees the curve of a building, high windows. Why can't they leave it like that, she wonders, put in a little park maybe, but the land is too valuable. Something else will be raised up, something not as good as air and sky. A homeless person is sleeping or lying, wrapped in a blanket and cardboard boxes, only his feet exposed, and he could be dead and they would not notice, all the people walking by (her life is one long freedom). In years to come people will ask, how could you ignore it, do nothing? And they will say, you don't understand, it was different then. What lies. The tram clangs as it squeezes round the corner. It seems a bit of wonder, all these people moving across the city.

Her mother had always hated Dublin, had begrudged it for the way it blundered along, a bit grubby, a bit corrupt, a bit beautiful. In her last days in the hospital, she had imagined herself back in Wexford, had said, 'Look, you can see the sea,' gesturing to the windows. 'It's sunny.' And Ruth had agreed, though it was grey out and you could only see the car park. Still, it was nice to be by a window and Ruth had sat, ignoring the pictures of the Virgin on every wall, and laid her hand over her mother's. It felt unnatural, really, given how little they had touched in life, but Ruth felt it was appropriate. Touch. Aidan had said, 'You can tell her, speak to her, don't let her go without saying the important things.' But when her mother had looked up at her and said, 'I think I'm on the way out,' Ruth had shushed her, had said something vague about getting better, and the lie had left them awkward again.

She had only gone down to the canteen for a sandwich,

had only been gone half an hour, but her mother had lapsed into a coma. Ruth sat beside her unconscious body, and said, 'I forgive you,' and, 'I love you,' words that were unimaginable in real life. And in those hours of silence, she had intoned to herself, my mother is dying. But that was unreal too.

She had told the nurses no priest and when she'd left that evening had asked them to phone her only if there was a major change. The call came at 4 am. The taxi through empty streets, the run through deserted corridors, and the sense, all along, that she had failed the test. Her mother had not looked peaceful, not really, and this had agitated Ruth. The doctor came to certify the death, and Ruth wanted to ask, is she really gone? As if she might suddenly open her eyes. But the doctor only offered her condolences, and Ruth, taking the plastic bag of belongings, had gone home an orphan.

Ruth weaves past the people standing outside the jeweller's, the baker's, the stationer's. It feels relentless. The Kilkenny shop, another brown building, perhaps lunch here, soup and a wholemeal scone, a classic. It looks busy, though, the window above full, the view of the college attracting every middle-aged woman in the vicinity. Ruth keeps going. Kildare Street. The Alliance Française, but she and Aidan had gone to the café there too many times. Go on, because she doesn't want to, can't, think about – *no, think of anything else*. Have a Brew-baker maybe? Café after café, on and on the choices and none of them are right. And here you are, this is what they did with the old street, knocked it down and turned it into glass and concrete and even when you look up, no variation, no beauty.

Ruth is aching, and any sensible person would say that she is hungry and nervous and tired, and that her day is a shitstorm, and she should just give herself a break. At some point, though, you have to take responsibility. 'You', what a classic distancing device, the client who always says 'you'. Ciara was like that, saying 'you' when she meant 'me', and it is not pleasant, this feeling of transference, that Ruth has seen herself reflected. (*Run! Stay!*) She has to face it, but how could you when there was a chain of events, when there was not just you, there were at least two of you making the mess? She passes the area railings at the start of Clare Street, which was only a few buildings, really. The gallery ahead. The hospital. It is just a check-up. Ruth keeps walking.

There is a rhythm, a unity to handing unwanted objects to strangers, the leaflet is like a connection and a barrier between you. It is a constant stream, but not too many, they are mostly businesslike, some pushing buggies or carrying shopping (mainly women), one person in a wheelchair navigates the broken pavement edge. 'Do you care about climate change?' Alice says over and over. Pen basically just holds a leaflet out any time someone walks near her. It's hard to care, say the people's faces, they are busy, they are going somewhere, they have their own problems, they think they can choose for air and water and earth not to be their issue. But they seem to like Alice, they smile as they look past her, as they swerve to avoid, shaking heads but nicely (Pen decides). A man in a suit pauses, rifles in his pocket, tries to hand them change.

'We're not collecting,' Alice says.

'We're interested in real change,' Pen hears herself say. The man walks on.

'Nice one,' Alice says, and Pen might explode.

'Do you care about real change?' Alice asks of the next few people. Pen thinks she could do this for ever, with Alice. Alice says perhaps they should branch out, maybe if they stood nearer the college they'd get, like, more young people? Pen nods. Alice once said that she likes how Pen's quietness makes her easy to be with. Pen hopes she meant it. Today-the-words-will-flow is proving harder than she'd thought.

They have only got as far as the Hansel and Gretel bakery, which looks like a really nice bakery, but it is still a slightly weird thing to call it because of how the parents were trying to lose their kids and the way the gingerbread and all the treats nearly killed them. Claire is not into stories with witches. 'For goodness' sake,' Sandy says, 'you don't have to feel sorry for everyone.' But Pen understands what her mother means, because she thinks maybe the witch was just not a people person and it doesn't seem fair to turn being an introvert into being a child-killer. 'It's not literal,' Sandy says, but Pen thinks, what if it is?

Pen says, 'Maybe they have students handing stuff out at the college already?' and Alice's face looks like it's sad, but then Pen says, 'At the corner we can see more of what's going on, and there's the cross-traffic.' So they drift back again to the edge of the square. Pen actually just likes how the pavement is bigger and there's fewer cars and there's more sky and somehow more air here. 'Trinity Ward', the wall plaque says. She feels slightly bad for tricking Alice.

'Do you care about real change?' asks Alice.

A woman in a blue coat takes a leaflet and actually stops to read, just on the edge of the kerb. She doesn't crumple it or let it fall, she reads. She turns back to them. 'Does this stress you out?' she asks. Alice says to the woman that they're taking back control, that's what this action is about, it's much more stressful not doing anything. She asks the woman if she wants to join them, but she says she has a meeting, she has a thing. She gestures ahead, her face white. She seems, to Pen, as if she is very sad and Pen imagines a large grey backpack. 'Thanks, though.' Halfway across the road, the woman suddenly turns and calls back. 'Can I take your photo?'

12.45 pm

Stepping off the kerb into Merrion Square, Ruth regrets the urge to get away, and turns on impulse. 'Can I take your photo?' The girls are looking at her, looking at each other. 'I can put it on social media or something, so more people will know.' It sounds a bit unlikely, even as she says it. What is it about these two girls that has captured her, made her step out of herself?

'Okay,' says the taller girl, nodding at the ground.

'Maybe,' says the younger-looking one, pointing to the banner at the top of the square, 'if you take that, and we're, we're in the foreground?'

'Much better idea,' Ruth says, committed now to this strange act.

The girls move into frame, Ruth takes a couple of shots.

'Do you want me to tag you or something?' she asks.

'Em, we're kind of meant to be in school,' the younger one smiles.

'Of course. Sorry.' Ruth is already backing away, waving her leaflet. 'Good luck, you're doing it for all of us.'

For a moment, the girls look pleased, and so Ruth is pleased too, with having stopped, with taking this snap, with acting on her feeling. Though really should she be photographing teenagers? Doesn't she have bigger things to worry about? Ruth crosses to the other side, looks back to check they're okay, but the girls are handing out leaflets again. She'll delete it, this photo that is mostly brown pavement and dark buildings and a corner of sky, and two girls, one in a bobble hat.

The railings of the park scroll by. In summer, on weekends, people come with their art, for sale, or just for show, tying the paintings to the railings, draped with plastic in case of rain, sitting on those folding stools. Ruth and Aidan have walked along here so many times, looking, appraising what they saw. What happened to all those paintings, were they in people's houses, strewn across the world?

Ahead there is a small group. They're standing in a semicircle, reciting something, what is it, some kind of poetry group? She's closer now and Ruth can see, it's not poetry, of course not. They are holding bibles. One woman, in reflective gear, a bicycle leaning beside her, leads the recitation, her tone high and strong. Another woman, a crucifix dangling from her wrist, is gently rocking with devoted concentration. Ruth is closer still and she sees one of the men is holding a photograph of a baby. *Oh.* Realisation hits her. It is for that they rock, their bodies angled towards the hospital. She cannot pass them. Ruth slows her pace, she'll have to cross to get around them. At least they don't have those tiny white coffins, god, what would that sight do to her, the thing you try most in the world not to think about. The traffic is thick here, the cars conspiring to keep her on this pavement, and all Ruth wants now is to get away. *Run!* She has no choice. She rushes past, rushes past, does not speak or glance or pause.

Finally, a break in the traffic, and there is a sign for a café, under the German institute. Ruth will not think about the other (*she is just hungry / nervous / tired*). Down the steps and thankfully no queue. Inside white and bright.

'What can I get you?'

The woman points to the chalkboard in front of Ruth, a list of sandwiches. She picks the first one.

'Chicken, sriracha mayo, good choice.'

Hard not to feel like she has been saved, a little.

'Anything to drink?' asks the woman, giving her a small train with a number on it.

Shake of head.

'Cash or tap?'

Ruth waves her card above the machine. She has not much loose change for the tip, a euro only, and shrugs apologetically.

There are couples at other tables and, who knows, they might be lovers, that man leaning towards the woman, or the two women, their heads together, who was fucking who? The ordinariness of it on the outside, the other life you carried on the inside. I am just tired, I am just very tired. A whole year, no, more, of being hungry / nervous / tired. Saliva in her mouth, food is coming soon.

The waitress comes bearing her sandwich. Salvation, again. Ruth eats and thinks that she likes this room, the café with its windows to the garden, she wonders if in summer you can eat outside. Above there are floors of white walls and high ceilings and windows to the park. Maybe Aidan would like it, but no, she cannot let herself imagine that. The chicken is tasty, good, and Ruth thinks again of being vegetarian. It wasn't justifiable, really, eating other living things. But then it feels overwhelming to consider all your life choices at every meal. Maybe those two girls were vegan, maybe they would save them all. The long trestle tables are filling up, Ruth resists the reflex to check her watch. There is still time.

Six months ago, April, she had begun bleeding. Begun bleeding when she shouldn't, smears on toilet paper, in her underwear, then a bit more, a dark red-brown viscosity she did not recognise. Before, she would have brought it to Aidan, her body an appeal, but now, well – *no*. Besides, it had seemed a little thing, had stopped for a while.

And then the bleeding had worsened in June, unignorable now, and so she had had to take her body and describe it, unfold it, expose it for her husband, though he no longer cared for it. 'I'm bleeding,' she'd said, and he had barely managed to make his face look interested, so that Ruth wanted to shout, 'I'm dying!' just to see if the reaction varied. Something must have shown in her face, because he said, 'Sorry, I don't know what—' but Ruth had turned away. 'You don't give me a chance,' Aidan objected later when she'd said that, on the off chance he was interested, she'd made an appointment with the GP for the next day. The GP had said it was probably fibroids, they were benign in most cases, and she had only 'a mild concern'. But the shadow of something was in the room anyway, and Ruth went home and said 'fibroids', the word proof of something, finally, wrong with her. And it was only then that Ruth had looked at the appointment letter, the referral to Holles Street maternity hospital. 'Why go there?' Aidan had demanded. 'Why not be referred elsewhere?' And she could not bear to say that in the gush of fear she hadn't noticed.

'Can I get you anything else?' Ruth's plate is empty so she will have a coffee, if only to delay the waiting room a bit. The gynaecologist had been all efficiency in July, breezy even, a quality Ruth had found both reassuring and confusing. No need for an operation or anything like that, she'd been told, and so she collected the prescription and went home, took the pills and watched her body return to normal.

Ruth's latte is borne aloft now by a waiter who grins as he delivers it. Ruth does not like coffee much, but it is better than tea 'out', that had been her mother's thing. Getting tea 'out' where you couldn't ensure the water was just boiled or scald the pot or choose the mug, that was bad tea, and Ruth cannot shake it, her mother's rightness about tea at least. In July, flush with her unexpected sense of relief, Ruth had gone back to her yoga practice, had decided to meditate before breakfast, to eat well, to breathe deeply. Aidan had not been as enamoured of the plan, of her declarations of newness, and perhaps she should have known. You can't just start a marriage again.

'The bear went over the mountain,' Aidan had sung at her in a moment of cruel insight, because she had told him, oh, years ago when they were new and still learning each other, she had told him of that family holiday. It was a long car journey, she must have been about five, and she'd sung (delighted with herself), over and over, the song about the bear going over the mountain to see what he could see. But her mother had hated it, told her to shut up, and when Ruth had kept going, she had stopped the car, made her get out, told her to stand by the side of the road, 'Don't move, now.' Ruth had not dared move, had only stood and watched as her mother had driven away. She'd come back, of course she had, but Ruth had learned her lesson. Aidan had not meant to bring all that up, 'I just meant,' and he sounded exasperated, not unlike her mother it had to be said, 'I just meant the way you're always chasing something, and when you can't find it, you change the goal. It's so simple for you.' Ruth had denied it, especially the swipe about it being simple because it was not, it did not feel simple at all. 'Protesting too much?' was all Aidan had said.

Ruth watches other people at the till, tapping their cards, and thinks how the bank will know that they were all here, in this room together, they will know what they ate, who they ate with. All the liaisons. Two women hovering by the counter glance over, their trains clutched against their coats, clearly gunning for her table. Ruth gathers her coat and bag, takes a deep breath. It is just a check-up.

1.05 pm

'Maybe we should head up to the gathering?'

Every time Alice says she really hopes there's, like, a massive crowd because then no one can ignore us, or that what we're saying is really serious, as if Pen doesn't know this, Pen agrees but secretly hopes there aren't the thousands Alice hopes for. The only problem with people is that they look at you and stand close to you and make noise, and Pen really wants to be around other people, she really does, but the idea of them and the reality are not the same and sometimes Pen feels like her whole self is being crushed by, well, other people. The *multitudo*.

But there aren't masses in the end. This street is closed off too and the Gardaí have bored faces on as they protect a line of cones, waving traffic away. Pen could do that job. They pass the red building on the corner, Pen saying 'Italianate' in her head. 'She may as well know what she's counting,' Sandy used to say to Claire. 'See, Pen,' Sandy drew a line from her up to the top of the column, 'see the monkeys? Can you see that they're playing billiards?' And Pen had nodded, but then Sandy looked at her, wanting more. Pen was paused, figuring out her response. But Sandy didn't wait, just turned and pointed it out for Soraya. 'Cool, Daddy!' Soraya was only ten but seemed to know the right thing to say.

The black gates of the Dáil are on their left and most of the people are gathered in front of them. Alice says, 'Yeah, cool,' when Pen points over to the crowd's edge. Pen's heart lifts because Alice makes her feel safe and like flying at the same time. From here they can see people in fluoro tops, people with loudspeakers and is that, yes, a giant pink boat. Up the front, by the gates, someone is shouting. Pen thinks that Alice would like to be further in. But then Alice wouldn't be here without her either, Pen knows that somehow too. There are banners floating over the crowd, more signs, and a huddle of people in costumes. Maybe things are happening now, their bodies press together more. Bodies of oxygen, carbon, hydrogen and nitrogen. 'It's good to remember everyone is made of the same things,' Claire says, 'even if they're different in lots of other ways.'

Pen arranges her body in space, feeling her toes in her shoes, her feet on the ground, the tendons connecting her limbs, her bones stacked, head over heart, she's tall, at least that gives her breathing space. Will Alice hear her if she does her breathing, but there's noise up ahead now, vague at first, in through the nose, out through the mouth, it sounds like 'our right to survive'. Alice grins round at her, her mouth moving along to the noise. Now is the moment. Don't overthink it, that's the trick, and Pen hasn't and afterwards she can't say exactly what she did, but her arm must have moved and now she is holding Alice's hand. Pen feels it in her body, this wave, and it is what feeling happy feels like.

A giant skeleton floats by the gates, and there's more shouting, and Pen can see big cameras at the front too, and maybe they'll want her to wave a banner and if they ask her to, she will breathe in and out, and say, 'Yeah, cool.' It will be easy, it will all come easy. Alice is shining, she's always shining, and Pen is shining too.

There are two camps, believers and non-believers. Alice is a believer, Pen is a believer. That's why they are here, holding hands. They are holding hands. And though Pen recognises the numb-feeling in her head, she won't say it to Alice because then she would lose this other feeling, and lose this moment, which as private as it is, as hallowed as it is in Pen's mind and heart and tendons, can only happen, is only happening, because they are in this crowd, because they can disappear. The chant goes on and Pen is part of it all.

Everyone is looking at the coffin now, being carried high at the front. It's too late. It's not too late. That's what the coffin means. The whistles are shrill, not a kind sound, a warning, and it goes through Pen, not just her head, her whole body, a kind of alarm. Pen winces and Alice squeezes her hand. It's okay.

Alice is smaller and she's on tippy-toes trying to see, she asks, 'What does it say on the boat?'

' "Tell the Truth",' Pen says, relieved to have something she can do for Alice.

Near the gates, the performance of death over, the coffin is lifted and they are moving, flags waving, more whistles, like they're dogs, like maybe their spirits are flagging, exhausted by death and hope and anger, and so they need to move. It is a slow pace on the edge, fine for Pen, she likes to have time to look at the world, but Alice's fingers slip ahead so she speeds up too.

'Hi, Pen! Pen, right?'

Alice lets go.

Jo is there, standing in front of them, with a poster on a stick, 'Act Now', and a big face close to her, reaching out her hand to Pen's hand, which is free because Alice let go, and Jo shakes Pen's hand and lets it fall and now it's empty. Alice is saying, 'Hi, I'm Alice, yeah, it's so cool to be here. We handed out leaflets earlier.' And then Alice looks embarrassed. Jo has an extra placard (it's a placard, not a poster on a stick, you're so stupid, Pen), an hourglass sign with 'Tell the Truth' on it too. Alice beams, she'd be proud to carry it, 'Yeah, brilliant.' Jo is asking do they know anyone, is Pen's mum here, but no, she's working, course, yeah, she's cool, as a lecturer, she's cool, she's political.

They're nearly at the end of the street now, the crowd viscous as the corner comes, Jo and Alice talking, chatting, no, talking and laughing, no, laughing and chanting. Can't drink oil, keep it in the soil, as slogans go it's not a classic, because to really mean something it has to be true, and no one would try to drink oil. Pen's mother has a reusable glass cup, looks shocked if she's offered plastic, but she's not actually, no one is, actually, drinking oil.

Past the museum where the bog bodies are (carbon too) and the Viking hoard with the tiny gold boat, which has tiny gold oars, and tiny gold benches, and what would the Vikings think of Dubh Linn now, that's what Sandy says. Pen doesn't know and the crowd won't let her think about it. There is a pulse in her head. And the light is changing.

As the crowd rounds the corner, the world seems at once too close and then very far away. Pen concentrates on the edges: the pavement edge, where the concrete meets the tarmac, the way it's bordered with stone at the corner itself, the way it's rounded and dipped for people to cross. Keep moving. Across the road the traffic lights, then the wider pavement with people walking there too, more space between them. Pen wishes she was over there, as the crowd she is in presses closer.

Observation, Pen. Away, away, she thinks, breathing, looking elsewhere.

The railings of the park (Stephen's Green, Pen, you know this!) run along the pavement edge, lined with bushes and trees that cast a deeper shadow. Beyond the trees, Pen knows, are ponds and green spaces and fountains. If Pen lets go of where she is, of the press and pull, she can be there again, with Claire and Soraya. Sustaining. Can hear Claire calling to her sister to be careful as she tries to balance on the thin low metal rails that go around, that contain, the grass. Soraya is better than her at playing too. Pen is not good at balancing, can still remember falling from something when she was small (a wall?), the sensation of being lost, the hospital and the crutches and her father shouting 'clumsy child syndrome' over and over. Pen's mind swerves. The trees, they spread their branches over the grass where you can sit safe in the shade. The line, what was it? 'Annihilating all that's made / To a green thought in a green shade.' The sun. Its heat. Is it a trick of the light, what Pen sees now?

These things happen elsewhere.

But Pen sees it. *Apocalypsis.*

This is her vision: the greenness will turn into grey, bleaching and dying under an orange sky that means only heat and death and air so terrible nothing can breathe. The ground will be brown and dusty, they will try to revive it but then they will have to stop, to save other things. They will say phrases like 'mass forest die-offs' and 'desertification' as if it's normal. The death will be invisible at first, as air bubbles invade the trees, cracking open their delicate, watery veins. They will only really notice when all the trees, all the sycamore, the holly, the hawthorn, the plane, dry and crack and fall. When the shelter starts to disappear. And they will wonder what a world without trees will mean and there will be photographs of what trees used to look like. It will be scorched earth then, salted soil, dead birds and animals, not just this park, oh no, it will happen to all parks, all gardens, all green places. They will watch plains flood, lands become abandoned, air become brown. Water become brackish. It will all be lost. They will all be destroyed. Corpsed.

But no one else sees this. No one else feels it. Not here, not right now. Pen's vision clears a bit, so that the darkness at the edges and the wind and the hot sun recede and the noise in her head is not the cracking trees but her blaring thoughts again, and her feet are on the street again, and as they turn into Merrion Street the future is the future again. Only damp green leaves now and grey skies, the 'Reserved' sign on the old bank building as too many people to count (the numbers will be disputed) do this march, which is basically just a slow walk, as they follow a pink boat from one big building to the next. 'It's not a government, it's a faceless corporation,' says a man walking near Pen. (Why do they say faceless when they mean uncaring?) Pen thinks of all the people in those buildings, and how to them, rather than to others, is given the management of the world.

It is too late. Nothing they do will matter.

They are just in time. This could make the difference.

Alice let go of Pen's hand.

2.00 pm

At the Holles Street entrance Ruth does not need to ask directions from the porters, she knows her way through the double doors and right down the corridor. She checks in with the receptionist, 'Gynae?' she asks, and when Ruth nods, tells her that she's sorry, there may be a bit of a wait, it's busy today. 'You know where the waiting room is?' Ruth does. There are girls with their mothers and a few women, just staring ahead, or looking at phones, no guessing what each of them is in for. Some women, some wombs, some people were lucky, and some weren't, and there was no good reason why, which wasn't enough of an explanation, really, didn't satisfy the need you had for an answer, but you had to accept it somehow. Two floors upstairs other people are having babies.

Ruth stares ahead because the worst thing you can do in a waiting room like this (and it is narrow, she could almost touch the knee of the woman across from her), the worst thing is to catch someone's eye, to share that tight grin that says, I see you and you see me and we will pretend that we do not see each other, that we do not share this thing inside us. A nurse appears at the doorway and they all look up in hope and fear, until she gestures to a teen who, rising in tandem with her mother, goes out wordlessly. Ruth wills her name to be called.

The morning of the D&C she and Aidan had followed the nurse to the far end of a ward, women lying in the other beds, and as Ruth had put the gown on, she had heard someone crying. She'd been nil by mouth. 'Suffers from low blood sugar,' she'd heard Aidan say to the nurse, so they had put in a drip to stop her from fainting. She had watched the anaesthetist count her down, she couldn't remember past eight, suddenly the world was just gone. And then the recovery room swam into focus, her mouth dry, and she'd moved her head only a little, but she must have made a noise because a nurse was there, minding her, and then she was up in the ward. The connecting scene was gone from her, they must have wheeled her through the green corridors, and then into the bright ward, where the nurse had asked if she wanted tea and toast and they were very sympathetic, really, but she was somehow untouchable.

'Ruth Ryan?' Ruth sighs because she didn't have to wait that long after all, and she sees the other women think, lucky her, poor her, as she dutifully gets up and follows the nurse. She tries to enter the doctor's room smiling, because you have to pretend you don't hate this, don't hate sitting in your coat, too hot, too female, too scared to say anything other than 'yes' and 'no'. It must be strange for the doctor too, strange to have only patients with vaginas, strange to say, 'If you could just undress,' to a parade of women, strange to have to pretend you can't see their shame. Ruth answers all her questions right, so she is given a gown. Behind a curtain she takes off her coat, her shoes, her trousers, her socks, her pants, arranges the gown over her, says, 'Okay.' The doctor pulls back the curtain, the nurse at her shoulder. The doctor smiles, the nurse smiles, but not at her.

Ruth, lying on the paper sheet on the pleather bed, tenses slightly as it reclines. The doctor lifts her feet into the stirrups. Ruth is wide open now. Look at the ceiling, look at the wall, look at the top of the doctor's head as she bends in, try to make conversation as if your vagina is not hanging open for all to see. They have to do this, winch your legs open, because the body protects its secrets.

'A vaginal ultrasound just gives us a lot more information,' the doctor's tone is apologetic. 'Sorry, there can be a little discomfort if you're tense.'

Ruth could tell the doctor that she's had countless internal exams, but she's not meant to be the expert in the room.

'Yell if you need to,' says the doctor, smiling over her shoulder as she puts freshly washed hands into gloves, and they snap over her arms. 'We've heard it all.'

The scope goes in. *It's just a check-up*, Ruth tells herself, *the bleeding has stopped*, as she feels it making its progress into her, not as bad as a speculum even.

'I see,' the doctor pauses, looking at the screen, and Ruth tenses for real this time. 'No, you can relax,' the doctor says, patting Ruth's leg, and Ruth has to restrain an urge to kick her. 'Intramural fibroids shrunk,' the doctor says almost sotto voce to the nurse. Then, looking at Ruth, 'You've had no smelly vaginal discharge or pelvic pain since?'

Ruth agrees she has not.

And now the doctor is pulling out the tube, wiping it down, yanking off her gloves. 'You might get a tiny bit of bleeding, just a light spotting.'

Ruth remembers the doctor had said that to Aidan when he was taking her home from here, from upstairs, and Aidan had said, 'What is spotting?' and Ruth had thought, how different we are, how much more blood there is in my life. The nurse hands her a sanitary towel and Ruth is suddenly, crushingly, grateful for this wordless kindness. And then she is pulling on her clothes again behind the flimsy curtain, rushing her socks, pushing feet into shoes, determined to be a person again.

The nurse is gone when she emerges and as Ruth half-sits down at the desk the doctor waves her hand and says, 'You're good to go – I'm sure you'd like to never see me again!'

'Right, okay,' Ruth hesitates at the door, feeling slightly faint.

The doctor looks up. 'Unless there's anything else?'

'No,' Ruth shakes her head a little. 'Thanks.'

Back out to the linoleum corridor and the smell of the hospital. In the foyer, though, the faint feeling persists, and Ruth has to sit down. It is better, this dismissal, she thinks, than the silence and delay which mean bad news. She leans her head back, closes her eyes, allows the lightness in her brain to take her for a moment. Things to be grateful for: no more growth, no more bleeding. Not cancer. Ruth hates gratitude lists. Hates how exhausting they are, rehearsing all the reasons why you weren't meant to be angry. With her eyes closed Ruth hears the bustle of the hospital and fears she might vomit.

'Is someone getting you a taxi?' asks a concerned voice and Ruth opens her eyes to see a woman sitting a few chairs away. She has a baby in a car seat on the bench next to her, between them, and suddenly Ruth can't bear it. She half-shakes, half-nods her head. A man comes through the door and the woman turns, smiles and looks up at him. She begins to get up but she can barely stand, so he bends to kiss her, and in that split second, Ruth could grab the car-seat handle and take the newborn with her. It would be so easy. Instead, she watches as the man picks up his child and the mother leans on his arm and they go out, a family. And Aidan was right, she should have asked for a referral to another hospital.

Ruth looks down at her phone, but the screen is blank. Aidan, with all his time for thinking, had not said anything last night or texted today, nothing to show he remembered her appointment, no wishing her luck. Ruth remembers the wave of relief three months ago when they'd said, 'It's just fibroids.' And how she had thought, what does it matter if my womb hasn't given the world babies, when it isn't going to kill me. But this feeling was hard to translate into words, impossible to say to Aidan. She had come home that day in July, waving the prescription, and said, 'I'm not dying.' Expecting what? Hoping what? Aidan had said, what had he said? Something about being pleased for her. As if it was not for him too. As if this was not something they shared. Perhaps it had been too much for her husband, her sudden happiness, her declaration that this time the doctors could cure the thing that was wrong inside her.

Ruth is out again, in the air, turning back up to the square. A young man steps onto the pavement in front of her, shooing a small boy ahead of him. 'Daddy?' the boy says, turning, and Ruth wonders if the man, who can't be more than twenty, can really be a father himself. Ahead two girls turn to look, to smile at the boy. The young man shoos him again and walks back the way he came. The boy, his hand taken by one of the girls, who might be his mother, looks back, asking, 'Where is Daddy going?' and it seems as if there will be tears. But the mother (is she?) bends down, saying, 'He's coming,' and this pacifies the child. Ruth passes them as they dawdle on the corner, catching the happy smile on the boy's small face. So simple. The person you love is coming.

Of course, Aidan had cared, had been relieved about the fibroids diagnosis. She is being unfair to him by remembering how blank his face had been when she'd said it first, about how she was bleeding. Weighting her case against him, so she does not have to feel so sick at herself.

Ruth steps into the park (no sign of the zealots, thank god). She is not meeting Lisa until three, fifteen minutes yet.

2.25 pm

Pen watches.

It is urgent, apparently, what Jo is saying, Alice needs to know, they bend heads together. Up ahead, beyond the multitude, there are speeches, a makeshift stage. A girl declares that they only have one planet, it's her future, collective responsibility, leadership. Alice should be listening, but she's – she is leaning into Jo. Pen watches. The announcer thanks the girl, says, 'And Annemarie is only eight!' At eight Pen was being sent out of class, at twelve she was being given medication that made her feel like a lump of lead, at fourteen she was being asked if she wanted to go to a different school. 'No way,' said Claire. Pen wonders if Annemarie's mother is proud.

After last year, at Lauren's house, Pen's mum had come to get her. 'What happened?' she'd demanded, and it sounded wrong to say, they put me in the wardrobe, because they hadn't even forced her, they'd just said, do it, and she had. At first it had been okay, it was just small, it was just dark. But in the dark it had got hot and she'd heard noises, them laughing maybe, but it could have been inside her head, and it was too hard to breathe so she had started making that low noise. They'd opened the door and she'd fallen out onto the floor, groaning. Pen remembers their faces, Chloe was crying and saying, 'I never wanted to, I didn't want to do it.'

Alice is clapping, but what for, she hasn't listened. Alice

gets criticised in class too, she stares out the window or doodles in her jotter. But no one calls Alice 'special'. Pen is special so she has to sit in the front, to avoid overload, near the door. She gets two timeouts a day in case she needs to go into the corridor, to breathe, and feel her feet on the floor, touch the wall, count the notices on the board, spell out each word in her head. But she hardly ever needs to, she wants people to see this, that she is managing. There is no normal, says Claire, but Pen will be normal if it kills her.

The video had gone up online and it had 367 views. Which was not so much in internet scale, and Sandy said, 'Just don't watch it!' like Pen watching it was the problem, and not strangers, or people in the school. Had Alice watched it? Pen's stomach twists. In the video Pen's face had been all red and there were snots and tears on her cheeks and her whole body was convulsing. 367 views. And that was over a year ago, how many views now? Thinking that question makes Pen feel again the sensation she had when she stood in the bathroom of their old house, running her finger over the edge of her mum's razor, watching the skin as it turned white when she pressed down against the blade. 'Too thin-skinned,' she heard her dad's voice echo.

Pen wants to take Alice's hand, to say, let's run, let's go, let's be on our own! Is it worse to think of it, her and Alice running, laughing through the streets, free together, no destination or plan or strategy, only themselves, is it worse to think of this and know it is impossible for so many reasons, or never to have the idea or the impulse?

A politician is talking now, congratulating them all for coming out, people are making sacrifices he says, it is for our children. Claire always gets angry when politicians say things about 'our children', or being parents, 'As if being a parent gave you special powers.' Claire would tear up the flyers that came in the door, because apparently being a parent could make you proud and angry at the same time. What should Pen think about this politician, who may or may not be a parent, when he says 'children' like it's a code word? Which children does he even mean? All of them, or do only-some-count?

Pen can't imagine ever wanting to have children. She knows her body will do what it wants whatever she feels, not even a meltdown can stop it. Release and shed, release and shed (*purgationes menstruae*). Pen is happy to see the blood (though it is not blood) wash out of her. She does not want to be told that she will change-your-mind-when-you're-older. People go on about experience, but actually Pen knows, Alice knows, even-fucking-Annemarie knows, having less experience doesn't mean you know or see or understand less. It is the opposite.

Now the speeches are over, the clashing noise is going-going-going without a break, there are people bumping and laughing and touching. She wants to leave. Pen and Claire have a danger signal, Pen puts her hand on the top of her head, it looks a bit strange but less strange than throwing herself on the floor. Pen's hand is on her head now but here, on the march, it's probably a symbol of saying 'the climate' or 'vote for change'. Alice is still smiling. Alice has not seen her hand. Soon Pen will have to leave, which is the one thing she promised her mother she would not do, she would stay with Alice, with Jo, she would not get lost. But Alice is smiling and Jo is leaning and they are together now, you don't have to be an empath to know that. Pen whispers, 'Timeout,' and she's gone.

2.45 pm

'Who can tell me what the women are fleeing?' Claire looks at the class. They look back at her, or they look at their pens, dawdling across paper, or they look at their feet. It's nearly over, this hour, and still they have not really started. She should ask the question a different way. 'Why does Aeschylus choose to make the female chorus the main voice of the play?' Her questions are too abstract, you have to ask questions people actually want to answer.

Claire considers asking them what does 'suppliant' mean, but they will not know, she had to look it up herself. It is hard to know, looking at the bodies in front of her, how they see the world, what they want from it. She thinks of Pen, of how her daughter has taught her how to make space for others. Claire pauses, maybe she should give them a break from questions. 'Let's take five minutes to write up your reflections on that question, then we'll compare notes.'

This room has windows on two sides. Since the start of term there has been building work nearby so that Claire has to teach against the grinding noise of drills and machines. Hard to believe that in a couple of years Pen will be sitting in a classroom like this. They start off as these tiny little, well, aliens was the only word for it. Oh, you got used to it, this small being that needed you, that was an extension of you, and you learned to cherish the total dependence. But then, once you did, once you felt like maybe you had the hang of it, it was suddenly time to push them out into the world again. You have to hold back, let them be themselves, course you do. But that doesn't mean you don't ask yourself why it's always your daughter standing by herself in the playground. Claire knows the reasons now, is ashamed of how long it took her to see. Her lovely girl. Her difficult girl. Pen who has a sense for when others are struggling. Pen who brings her whole self into everything. Pen who cannot *unfold*. And it is like she is tiny again, like Claire has to learn her all over again.

Sometimes Claire pretends to read through her notes, to give the students a break from her attention. Today she can't even manage that, her feeling for Pen ticking away at the back of her mind. A day off from school is not like Pen, she loves her steady routine. But then Claire has never seen her so happy, just being with Alice does that. Oh, she could still be a pain, still get in a fury and throw things, still shut down. How many times has Claire wished she could escape from the worry, the guilt. That she could walk away, even for five minutes. But then she feels guilty for even wishing that much.

Claire checks her watch, glances at the bent heads before her. Another minute won't hurt them. She had always hoped to raise her daughters to be strong, and it is just a shame that she has had to do it alone. Sandy's not all bad, but he's old-fashioned, to the point of being stuck. 'You're only forty-five, not medieval,' she had shouted as he had shrugged, consigning his first daughter to the rubbish heap. *Oh, Sandy*, but she is tired of the question and tired of the answers. She is done looking back. A whole life of her own. It meant coming home alone, it meant making decisions alone, it meant lying in bed alone. But loneliness has its compensations.

'Okay, time up.' The class looks up at her. 'For our last few minutes, I'd like to consider why the theatre company recruits the players from the community. Why not use professional actors?' Claire had taken Pen to see the play last year at the festival, and it had been quite something to sit in the audience and know that most of the actors onstage were just ordinary people. Pen had liked it so much she said maybe she would learn Greek too, but Claire had enough on her hands with Latin springing up all over the place.

'Maybe it's so that we think refugees could be any of us?'

'Great point, so does anyone want to add to that, expand on it?'

'If the foreigners are us, then that implicates us.'

'Keep going, this is great.'

Claire had told Sandy she thought perhaps Pen and Alice might be more than friends, not imagining he would want to stop them from seeing each other so much, which was ridiculous (medieval!) but maybe it was true that you only really knew someone when you raised kids with them. Or not with, exactly. All the same, she needs to talk to her daughter. 'Be careful who you love,' she wants to say, because she sees Pen's hurt, sees her become her turtle self when her love is not returned. Her dad, Alice, whoever it is. Those fucking girls last year. Meltdown. Silence. The cutting. Dear god, the cutting. Then recovery and things okay for a while. The terrible cycle they are all, somehow, trapped in. And the only thing Claire can do is watch.

The class are talking now about the role of the audience, are they the suppliants or the *demos*? It's a good question. She likes them so much, these people who come together every week. I see you try, she wants to say.

2.45 pm

'I looked around and you were gone,' Alice says. Pen should have said something, should have told her, how was Alice supposed to know.

Because you're my best friend, Pen does not say, except with her eyes, which she can't focus anyway. Pen's hand holds the railings, her hand at the end of her arm, which rests in the shoulder socket, Pen has tight shoulders, she can't hold her arms out for long or she loses circulation to her hands, those hands which are holding on to this railing, which is painted black, which is cold. She can feel cold, that must be a good sign. Pen had put her head down, to breathe, to stop seeing the world, but she can look up now, can see the red houses, can see that she is near to where they had their photo taken. You're in the driver's seat, the woman-therapist would say. 'Called a timeout,' Pen says. 'Left you with Jo so you'd be safe.' It's more of a gasp than a statement, but it's words at least.

'Okay, but you have to tell me.' Alice is trying not to be annoyed with Pen for acting like she's alright when Alice, her best friend, knows she must have been panicking. Alice is annoyed with Pen for panicking, which she knows is a mean thing to think, but Alice doesn't want to be in charge. Truth is, Alice feels guilty. Because it was Jo who noticed Pen was gone, and Alice remembered too late her promise that they'd stand at the edge. She'd wanted to be absorbed by it, by the crowd, by something that was bigger. But now she is here and she has to do something and that something is take care of Pen. Perhaps they can try the gallery, it will be quiet. But then Alice worries that maybe they need a ticket?

Alice has to look after her. This is Pen's worst fear come true. She wanted Alice to see her, to want to be with her because she's special in the right ways. Pen doesn't want to be a crazy person. She isn't one because her mother-therapist-teachers-Alice tell her she isn't but it occurs to her, as Alice leads her by the hand, that all crazy people are actually just real people, and that those people feel exactly like her, and though they try to be not-crazy, in the end they still have episodes, and these episodes make their families sad, and that sadness is something no one can do anything to fix. So maybe what she means is that she doesn't want to be a person who makes other people sad.

They go through a set of railings and up a wide path and the building ahead has pillars and there doesn't seem to be anyone around which Pen registers in some part of her brain that is still working. In under the pillars. The building is quiet.

Safe-calm-contained.
Safe-calm-contained.
Safe-calm-contained.

They walk until they get to a room that's almost daylight because the roof is glass and really high up. Double height, Sandy would say. They sit on a bench, which is good because you can sit in galleries and not be weird, not be sick.

'It was just too much,' Alice murmurs, standing in front of her, shielding her.

It wasn't, Pen wants to say, it was you and Jo, and the dying-trees, that too, but it's all mixed up. She was okay but then she wasn't.

Alice looks up towards the roof light and wonders what comes next. Pen is calmer already, Alice can see that her face is less white, that she isn't muttering any more. But she doesn't know if this means it's over or not. Should she ring Pen's mother?

Pen is looking round her and at her, Alice, as Alice shifts from foot to foot. Alice's eyes are narrowed, that means worried, Alice is worried. How did she get here? She must have walked. Alice walked with her. This happens, her memory goes. This happens.

'Should I call your mother?'

Pen wants to say no but something else is going on and now she cannot remember how to breathe. How do you do that thing where you pull air into your body? No-air-no-lungs-no-breath. The world shrinks, there are black curtains coming in from the outside.

'Pen, Pen, are you okay?'

2.45 pm

In the square, Ruth hears a rumbling noise, boom boom, it must be a drum beat, though she can't see its source. Somewhere on the far side of the trees. She walks towards it, along the path that skirts the wide green space, the drums getting louder. Her clothes still feel strange on her, reminding her of the body underneath. Ruth will meet Lisa soon. Hard, no, impossible, to hide from her friend that something is wrong. But how much, what, to tell her? There are more people in the park than usual, and Ruth, not quite able for the next bit, takes a seat on a bench. Just for a moment. There are a few tents going up on the south side, a motley group of turquoise and green. Perhaps the rain will hold off for them. A few signs staked in the ground make her smile, 'Make love not CO_2'.

In April, before there was any bleeding, there had been — what? — a casual betrayal, far too casual. The task force on mental health had finished earlier than expected, and the EU delegates had thought they'd make the most of the afternoon. 'Discover Dublin,' they said, wondering if maybe they could go for a pint? Ruth was the native so it was only natural she would lead them. She'd headed for the Swan, thinking it would be empty at that time, and it would be a nice walk through the Green. The visitors had happily followed her, praising it all. They thought the bar was 'charming', especially when she told them it was named for an underground river. Ruth had enjoyed their enjoyment, had seen the wooden interior and big windows anew, had allowed herself to enter into the festivity of this unexpected weekday afternoon.

She had spoken to Lucas at the start of the day, but not again until she was standing next to him at the bar. He was quiet but obviously watching her, listening when she spoke, and Ruth had liked the attention. After a couple of pints, a few people wanted to hear traditional music and when Ruth had shrugged her shoulders, they had tapped into their phones and announced Slattery's and '*Rath*-mines', which they pronounced with the emphasis wrong. She texted Aidan: HOME LATER and he replied: HAVE FUN.

Rousing herself, Ruth walks again, following the path under the trees, from light to shade. There are more benches and a playground, a few children, a few parents. The boom boom goes on, slightly muffled by the trees.

They had got chips in Burdock's and then gone into the crowded bar, though you could barely hear the fiddle music above the din. He'd been talking to two other women, Italian perhaps, who looked up at him like the sun was about to emerge from his forehead, but he had kept glancing over at her, caught her eye a couple of times. Two people left their seats behind Ruth, just as Lucas came over to her. 'Do you want to see the snug?' Ruth asked. He was Danish, so had to have 'snug' explained to him. 'Intriguing,' he said as they settled on the bench, the half-door closed behind them. 'So, you are telling me in these Victorian times, women did not want to have a drink in public?' And Ruth had been just about to say that there were plenty of reasons for a bit of privacy, when a colleague poked in his head, 'Okay to come in?' Of course it was. What, really, had Ruth wanted to happen? She tried to make conversation, to explain again about Irish bars, but the beer suddenly felt flat in her stomach. It was a sign, she thought, to call it a night. She'd excused herself to the loo and then got her things, waved goodbye to the few left. Airily, as if they were friends, as if they often ran into each other in a crowded Dublin pub.

Outside the bar, on the corner, she had held out a hand for a taxi, watched the golden light approach, the car pull in. And then he had been there. 'Were you leaving without saying a goodbye?' Ruth had felt something then, and when he leaned in to hug her, she turned her mouth to his. They had kissed like teenagers. And Ruth had thought, oh, someone is kissing me, narrating it to herself as if it could not be real. He pulled away after a moment, but only to move his lips over her cheek and ear and neck, and it was so unexpected, this tender act. Over his shoulder she had seen the taxi idling, waiting to take her home.

Ruth has come to the far side, the war memorial by the gate. Is it for one war or, no, she sees the plaque, an offering to all the dead defenders. The flame moves in an invisible breeze. She feels dazed, and the drums are keeping pace now with her steps, or maybe she has fallen in with them. She pauses in the gateway and sees the Gardaí in their high-vis jackets and hears the pierce of a whistle. People are moving but without a focus and it must be the end of something, Ruth thinks, as she reads the signs and slogans being carried past. 'Act before it's too late.' Well, Ruth spends her professional life saying that in one form or another and is used to not being listened to.

She had come home. It was late, and Aidan had been asleep. 'Good night?' he murmured as she slipped into bed beside him. And Ruth had whispered, 'Yes,' but kept turned onto her side, away from him, the feeling still reverberating. *Someone wanted me.*

She feels another wave of faintness and tries to breathe more deeply, she is almost at the gallery door. 'Anything else?' the doctor had asked and perhaps there had been a moment, an opening, when Ruth might have said it, might have confessed, might have asked for what she needed. It was a small thing and a huge thing. Fix me. Because it is beyond her to heal herself. Fix me. Fix me. Fix me. The voices from the street are raised again, calling out for justice, but Ruth turns away.

2.55 pm

The woman's voice is calm. She asks Alice what their names are and nods as Alice talks. 'Alice and Pen,' she repeats. 'I'm Ruth.' And then the woman bends down, kneels down on the ground in front of Pen, and Alice says, 'She doesn't like to be touched, really,' but she sounds unsure suddenly. 'It's okay,' says the woman called Ruth. And then Alice says, 'She's, she's on the spectrum,' and imagines she sees Pen's eyes widen even more.

'Pen. You are safe. You're here. You're safe. Pen, can you close your eyes for me? That's right, close your eyes, gently. Good.'

And she has one of those voices that Alice thinks you would trust, you would follow, as if she knows you.

'Now, Pen, I know this will sound strange, but can you close your mouth for me? Yes, that's right, and keep it closed, keep your eyes closed too. Just listen to my voice. Now, Pen, keep your mouth closed and breathe in through your nose. And hold it for a second. That's right. And let it out through your nose again.'

The woman has a hand on each of Pen's shoulders.

'No, we're fine,' she says to the security guard who's standing there, asking about 999.

Alice manages a smile, trying to look casual so he knows they're not crazy people. 'She just got a bit hot,' says the woman called Ruth and he nods and walks away. The woman is holding Pen's shoulders still and saying, really softly, like a lullaby, 'In through your nose, and out again through your nose.' And Pen isn't making the wheezing noise any more.

'I'm going to ask you to stay still, just keep going in through your nose and now breathe out through your mouth. Good air in, old air out. Just let your body do its thing. It doesn't feel great right now, but remember – nothing can hurt you. In and out.'

The woman stops talking then, and just breathes along with Pen for a few moments. 'And can you slowly, carefully, open your eyes a little for me, Pen?'

The woman looks up and nods to Alice, with a half-smile, still holding Pen's shoulders. Alice sees how gentle she is and how she seems to know what to do and the right thing to say and Alice feels a wave of wanting to cry out to her, but her head is bent again towards Pen.

'Can you open your eyes, Pen, and just keep really still, just look down, no need to move. That's great. You're doing great.'

Look at me again, Alice could say. What do you see?

'Now, Pen, I want you to listen to my voice and my voice will guide you. You don't have to say anything, just listen to my voice. Breathe in through your nose, that's right, and now out through your mouth. Okay, you're doing really well, so we're going to take it slowly, and just go to the next step. Breathe in and listen to me, that's right, and out again. Can you name one thing you can feel? There's no need to speak, just name it in your head.'

A-woman's-hands.

'Have you got it in your mind? Great job. Now let's keep breathing. In through your nose, pause, out through your mouth, that's right. You're still safe. Okay, Pen, can you name to yourself two things you can hear?'

People-talking-somewhere-far-away-the-door-banging. Pen nods.

'You're doing really well. Now, deep breath again, breathe out, and Pen, can you name three things you can see?'

My-feet-the-floor-the-edge-of-my-glasses.

'Now, can you look at your hands, and notice one thing about them?'

They-are-not-shaking-any-more.

'Now, can you name one thing you can taste?'

Thirsty.

'You're doing great, Pen. Breathe in through your nose and pause, and out through your mouth. Okay?'

Pen's head moves a tiny bit, she wants to shrug the woman's hands off her. This is a good sign, she is coming back to herself.

'This is my number, I'll be in the gallery café for the next hour, so if you need anything at all, just call me.'

The woman is looking at Alice, then down at Pen's bent head, then at Alice again. Alice nods. She has only just recognised her, the woman who took the photo earlier.

'Anyone can get overwhelmed, there's a lot of noise out there.' Ruth smiles at Alice.

'Do you think I should call her mother?'

'It's really up to Pen. You guys are –' Ruth pauses. 'Are you eighteen yet?'

'We're both sixteen.'

'Okay, then. Yes, you should call.' Ruth hunkers down once more, whispering to Pen, 'You did great, Pen. It feels bad now, but this too shall pass.' She stands and smiles again at Alice. 'Will you be okay from here?'

Alice nods. She looks at Pen and when she looks around again, Ruth is walking away, looking back as she goes through under the arch, giving a small wave. Alice looks down, at her phone, at the card. It's hard to believe it was only ten minutes she was with them.

'Are you okay now?' Alice asks.

After feels terrible. There's a headache. Pen's whole body aches and she has to hold the phone to the side of her head and talk and it feels hard to do this. Pen hears Claire talking, 'Keep breathing, Pen. Can you focus on what you hear and keep your gaze on the floor or your hands?' Pen nods, and it is like her mum knows. 'Don't beat yourself up, Pen. I know you, I know you'll be embarrassed, but Alice cares about you.' Pen shakes her head, not wanting to hear, not wanting Alice to hear. What is Claire saying now? She's asking something. 'Can you say, "A dingo's got my baby"?' which is a line that always seems funny and Meryl Streep is the best actress and Pen almost smiles but that's too hard. 'How do you feel now, can you tell me one thing you are feeling in your body?'

'Aching.'

'Okay, well, that sounds like a premonition of what it feels like to be forty-five, which is painful but not actually fatal. Listen,' and Claire takes a breath, 'I don't want to ruin your day, but I think you should take this as a sign, listen to your body, head home.'

Pen sees her mother, sitting in her office, staring through the slatted blind at the wall she looks out on, surrounded by her books and papers and the hundred postcards of art by women she has taped to the walls, all the colours bleached to a blue palette by the west light.

'Coming home is not a failure, Pen.'

Claire sounds like she's trying to be reasonable, but Pen still says nothing.

'Fine,' Claire sighs.

Pen knows that 'fine' is the opposite of what Claire means, but sometimes Pen being a literalist is to her advantage, so she says 'okay' again.

'Okay, well, take it easy now, Pen. Get something to eat, promise me?'

'Yes, Mum.'

'I'll see you for dinner.'

'Okay,' Pen says, not because it's true but because she needs to stop talking now.

'Facts are your friend, Pen,' said the woman-therapist in their second session, and Pen wishes so hard she were here now, or Pen was in her calm, high-up therapy room now. Fact: she is not. Fact: she aches. Fact: hypoxia is what makes your muscles sore because they are straining so hard for oxygen. Fact: Pen and Alice skipped lunch, so Pen has low blood sugar and that's why the headache. Those are facts, and the facts are part of the reason why Pen feels terrible. But that's not the only reason her body feels like lead.

Alice is looking at the children's drawings, there's an 'art pod' in the corner of the atrium and some of the drawings are stuck up and Alice is looking at them. Alice is giving Pen space. Pen does not want this space because it is space between them, not space they are sharing.

It is an effort but Pen stands up, lets the dizziness pass, raises and drops her shoulders. Pen focuses on knowing where she is. Pen inhales. Pen walks over to Alice. And it is superhuman, and she is shaking again, and she has to remember how to breathe. She is standing next to Alice.

There is a moment then, Pen is paused, and Alice is paused, and perhaps neither of them is really breathing. And then Pen says something.

'Do you come here often?'

The girls will be fine. They have her number. Though it is hard not to feel guilty, leaving them like that. She'll be in the café, if they need her.

Lisa is there before her, at the counter, and just at this moment she twists her head round, sees Ruth coming into the atrium, and waves, 'Hello!' Lisa points at the cake display and then to two plates already in front of her, a slice of chocolate, a slice of lemon.

'Thanks,' Ruth says. 'You know me too well!' And Lisa turns and there on her front – nestled, is that the word? – is the baby. A bullet of panic in Ruth's stomach. Because she has not moved on, she has not lost her real longing.

'It's so great to see you!'

'And look,' Lisa gestures at the empty space around her, 'no buggy, hurrah!'

'That's great,' Ruth says, taking the tray. She follows Lisa to a table at the edge.

'God, though, it takes me about an hour just to leave the house and then I realise on the way I haven't even looked at my face.'

Ruth knows she has to say something. 'She's perfect, Lisa.' It's unmistakable, the glow of pride and love that emanates from her friend's face.

'Isn't she?'

If it was hard to see Lisa with a growing bump over the spring and summer, then this is far worse.

'I'll give you a hold later if you want, but she's just drifted off. I'm not sure if she'll even let me sit down. God, I'm starving, that's something they don't tell you. It's all, "Breast-feeding shifts the weight," but I am doing nothing but eating.'

Ruth smiles, 'No, you look great on it.'

'Stop, Zach has to say things like that, you I keep for your honesty.'

'Okay,' Ruth concedes, 'you look a bit tired.'

'Better,' Lisa nods, turning her attention to the cake.

Ruth takes a few bites herself, feels the sugar surge.

'You know,' Lisa says, 'there should be a rule that no marriages can break up within the first year of parenthood, just so no woman is afraid of eating or crying or farting her partner out of the place.' She pauses for comic effect. Then realises Ruth has frozen. 'Are you okay?' she asks.

'Oh, please,' Ruth says, 'not the counsellor voice.' And there must be something in her tone, because Lisa nods.

'I have those healthcare provider papers, let me give them to you while I remember. It's not an exaggeration when they say baby brain, though sleep-deprived human-slave brain, which no one fucking tells you either, is more like it. Here,' Lisa waves the pages, 'the cover letter says we just renew the terms. We're lucky, that solicitor did a good job on the practice agreement, it's fairly straightforward.'

Ruth remembers the man, his eagerness, his office full of stacked boxes. They had been unsure, nervous at the last moment, setting up on their own, had needed him to give them some seal of approval. How long does it take, Ruth wonders, before you feel like you know what you're doing?

'You're definitely coming back, then?'

Lisa looks surprised. 'What? Of course! I mean, I need the money to pay off the second mortgage from her,' she looks down again, her annoyance blatantly false. And Ruth remembers the tearful Friday nights over wine in Nealon's, the heartbreak of it all. Which they had shared until, well, Lisa and Zach had got lucky. There is a brief pause as both Lisa and Ruth gaze at the tiny, clenched hand just visible over the baby carrier. Baby fingers.

'I'm sorry, Ruth.'

'Yeah, me too.' Why could Lisa see what Aidan could not? That Ruth would have given anything for this. Except, and maybe Aidan had a point, she hadn't, had she? She had not given *anything*.

'I'm sorry, Ruth,' Lisa says again, 'are you okay?' Lisa looks at her friend and sees a flash of worry cross her face. Ruth hates to be caught. 'If you want to talk about it,' Lisa says, nodding towards her daughter's head, 'she'll sleep for a while yet.'

What is there to lose?

'I think Aidan might be leaving me.' There it is, said out loud, and for the first time today it feels real. Ruth checks her friend's face for corroboration. Lisa looks – what? – not particularly surprised.

'Oh Ruth, do you know, I mean—'

'There isn't anyone else, if that's what you're about to ask,' Ruth jumps in. Lisa shakes her head slightly.

'Then perhaps you're okay. Men only leave when they have a destination.' But even as Lisa pronounces this they both know, know Aidan, know his determination, that he would be the exception. Lisa shakes her head sadly, and like a reflex touches her baby's head, holds her a little tighter. As if divorce were contagious.

'Actually,' Ruth says, because it is annoying to see Lisa so obviously pitying her, 'I had a, a thing with someone.'

'An affair?'

And Ruth thinks again of that night, of the taxi idling, waiting to take her home.

'It was just, sorry, a one-off.' As if that made it okay.

Ruth had meant to go home, but he had kissed her neck. And, forgetting he was a stranger in the city, she had whispered, 'Is there somewhere we could go?' He had kissed her again and said, 'Perhaps my place?' In the taxi to his hotel, Ruth had suddenly felt awkward, but he had covered her hand with his and she'd felt that rush, again, the rush of being wanted.

'Who with? I mean, it doesn't matter,' Lisa has her head slightly to one side, enquiring.

'No one,' Ruth says. 'It was nothing. He was in town for a consultation process, Danish, never going to see him again.' Ruth waves her hand vaguely in the air, as if fucking someone who was not your husband was not a big deal. 'Maybe I'm a terrible person.'

'Maybe you're just human,' Lisa says, and Ruth feels a certain release. But Lisa looks distracted again.

'Oh,' Ruth says, the concern in her voice now, 'is she being sick?' But it's only drool, still the baby looks unhappy, red in the face. Lisa looks apologetic, pushes back her chair.

'Sorry, it's better if I stand and jog her a little,' Lisa is on her feet. But now the baby is beginning to cry, and Lisa says,

'I'm really sorry. If I do a circuit, she'll settle. I'll be back in a tick, I can really listen then.'

Lisa walks past the queue at the coffee dock, as if it is not extraordinary at all, as if it is so easy to do this, to make a person and carry them and mind them. She reaches the corridor, disappears under an arch, heads towards the foyer.

It was nothing. Not true.

In his room it had been awkward once more, until he had sat on the edge of the bed, and she had stood between his legs, bent down to him, and they had kissed again. Oh yes. And when he'd pushed his hands under her dress, she had pulled it over her head, taking off her bra too, so that he had said, 'Oh.' Ruth's mind had run a constant commentary of *Am I really doing this* until he had pushed her breasts together with his large hands and she felt it twang through her. And then it was like her body was leading and Ruth, whoever that was, was just following along with what this body wanted.

Ruth had climbed on top of him and then he had turned her onto her back, laid her down. His cock was soft, so soft she had wondered at first if he was turned on, but he had pushed inside her, and she had felt a heat, almost instant spasms. Ruth was surprised because that wasn't like her, but he was different, heavy on her, pushing her legs so wide she thought she might split but that was pleasure too. It was the opposite of what she liked with Aidan. But then, wasn't that why she had wanted it?

She had not come, though she'd been sighing so hard half the hotel must have thought she had. He had told her she smelled amazing. 'Amazing, amazing,' he kept saying it over and over. And Ruth had wanted to run her own hands over her skin, suddenly like silk, because her body was doing what she wanted it to do, it was not a failure, not defunct, it was a woman's body, it was her body.

Afterwards he had gone into the en suite and she'd lain with herself, slick in the aftermath. Then she heard him running the tap and the idea that he would wash his hands before coming back to touch her, it was ridiculous, but Ruth thinks that in that moment she had loved him.

Lisa, bouncing the baby on her chest, walks back under the arch and into the café area. 'I'm sorry,' she says, 'what a terrible time for me to leave, please let's talk about it some more, you were, you were . . .'

'I had a one-night stand,' Ruth says. 'My husband hates me, and my life is falling apart.'

'Mmm-hmm,' Lisa says. There is a tiny pause, Ruth starts it, breathing hard, then leaning forward, a paroxysm. Lisa's face is creasing too, 'No, no,' she seems to be saying, but it's hard to hear because they are both laughing so hard. A sound like a moan escapes Ruth's mouth. The tears come and they taste of salt marsh. Lisa is shaking her head. Because it is hysterical, it is unthinkable, Ruth's life can't be falling apart.

'Oh god, I'm sorry, worst friend ever,' Lisa gasps. Mercifully the baby has not woken. 'Do you think, sorry,' Lisa makes her face serious, 'do you think Aidan knows?'

Ruth shakes her head.

She had come home, showered but still with the burning sensation of another man on her skin, inside her. She had got into bed beside him, and he had woken long enough to ask, 'Good night?' and she had said, 'Yes,' and turned on her side, away from him. The real betrayal.

'Oh Lisa, it's not like I planned it,' though Ruth thinks, even as she says this, that this statement is not quite true either. That perhaps she had allowed herself to imagine – what? – that this stranger would carry her off, that this was the beginning of something, that it was, at the very least, a way out.

'You aren't the first,' Lisa pauses, her face looks like she is trying to find different words. 'I mean, you can't be the first couple to get a little . . . disoriented. After going through what you did.'

'Mmm-hmm,' Ruth says, not wanting to agree, though the truth of Lisa's comment is annoyingly obvious. 'It's just that Aidan hasn't touched me in so long, seriously, nothing I do is right for him, and he just freezes me out.'

'And what does Aidan do if you touch him?'

And Ruth shakes her head because for all her insight, Lisa is missing the point. 'It just felt really good to be touched by someone who wanted me for me.' God, she sounds like a little girl asking for a lollipop.

'Did Aidan say something to you this morning or is this a longer thing?'

How could Ruth have forgotten to say this bit?

'Aidan is at a conference, well, not "at" because the conference ended on Saturday, but he stayed in London for the weekend, to get . . . well,' and this also becomes real as she says it, 'to get a break from me.'

'He must be feeling lonely too.' Lisa sees Ruth wince, and it is not fair of her to push her friend like this, but it is a fact that Ruth is not the most sympathetic person. 'Did you ask him what was behind it all?'

Ruth shakes her head. Is this what you want, Aidan? It

would be so easy to ask. Yet she has not. Because not all pain comes in the shape of an affair.

'We used to laugh so much, you know,' Ruth redirects, 'and we never do any more. And part of me wonders, it feels like, like we've grown out of it.'

'Have you spoken to him today? Perhaps he's got it out of his system, the break was enough'?

Doubt suddenly floods Ruth, had he said he would be home tonight? She'd assumed so, but maybe not. Surely he had said, 'See you tomorrow'?

'Yes, I think he's home tonight. I guess,' Ruth says slowly, 'we'll have to talk about it all then.'

'Will you tell him about—'

'No.'

Lisa nods, 'Probably wisest. I mean, it was just a one-off.' The baby is stirring again, and Lisa sighs, rubs her little back, rocks the bundle slightly, 'You guys can make it through this. You have so much going for you, seriously.'

The baby starts to thrash, head moving from side to side, and Ruth wishes they had a few more minutes, perhaps then she could figure out the questions she needs to ask, so that Lisa could give her the solution.

Lisa stands and Ruth sees the tiredness on her, the way she has to ready herself for this small person's demands.

'Maybe she needs some air, to go home,' Ruth offers.

'Do you mind?' Lisa asks, looking apologetically at her friend.

But Ruth does not, and it will be a relief, actually, to have them gone.

Lisa layers up with coat and scarf and bag, 'I'm a glorified pack rat.' They try to hug around the lump of the baby.

'Keep in touch, let me know how it goes. You can talk to me at any time. I mean, I'm not sleeping anyway. Sorry, bad joke,' Lisa smiles grimly.

And Ruth thinks it is not just her, they are both bashful, now that Ruth's confession is out there.

'Don't worry,' Lisa smiles. 'You'll work it out. Isn't that what we say? Everything can be worked through.'

Ruth nods, and, reaching out her hand, she gently touches the baby's head.

'Sorry,' Lisa says, as she steps away, 'you never even got to hold her.'

4.00 pm

'Anything in your pockets, sir?'

Aidan shakes his head, scans the tray.

'And your shoes, sir.'

He looks at his feet, then up again at the security officer. Stupidly, he says, 'Shoes?'

The officer nods. 'In the tray, sir.'

There is always something you forget: belt, wallet, jacket, take your laptop out, liquids. Shoes. He bends to untie laces, then stands and pushes them off with his toes, a habit from childhood. At one point, airports had had a thing about umbrellas. All the weapons. Aidan drops his shoes into the tray, pushes it forward onto the conveyor.

'Step back, sir. Wait for the signal.'

Aidan steps out of the numbered circle, stands vaguely, waits for another nod from another security officer. Who waves him into the scanner.

'Hands above your head, sir.'

Aidan has never been called sir so many times in his life. Was it true the scans showed your body on a screen somewhere, should he care about this? What would it take for him to stop following instructions? As he steps out, Aidan sees that, mercifully, his tray has made it unscathed. Now there is the scramble to reassemble yourself. Why is it that putting your jacket back on always feels too hot on this side of security? Aidan casts a glance at the huddle of people waiting for the extra checks on their bags, feels a little grateful after all, and walks into the main terminal. It's slightly disconcerting to realise you're on a balcony, John Lewis to your left, the lights of Leon below. Aidan turns right, feels the relief as he pushes open the door of the airline lounge.

'May I see your boarding pass, sir?'

The Irish accent feels friendly, one of us, it says. Not that the English were rude or anything. Just English, he guessed, used to being more direct. Like Sophie, asking him out on Friday: 'I'd like to get to know you.' Perhaps it was just that she was younger.

'Do you know the lounge, sir?' Aidan nods that he does. 'Well, enjoy, and please remember that we don't call short-haul flights, so keep an eye on the board.'

'Thank you,' he says, pulling his case behind him, heading for the bigger armchairs near the window. It's almost empty and you have to wonder if they get the revenue to keep a large lounge like this. They save on the food, he guesses, just a few crackers and those mini-cheeses. Still, a full bar.

His phone had buzzed this morning, one of those reminders of the past, 'Discover 2 years ago', which he'd clicked on before thinking that maybe he didn't want to remember two years ago. But it was only a photo taken out of a plane window, impossible to know where. He thinks of the other photo he saw this morning, a status update. Blue-and-white swimsuit, large bump, a tagline that said, FOUR YEARS AND FOUR IVF CYCLES, FEELING VERY LUCKY.

Aidan gets up again, crosses to the kitchenette, takes a bottle of sparkling water out of the mini-fridge. Goes over to stand at the window. He should do something practical like get food for the plane. He should text Ruth, tell her he's on his way. But no, he'll only be interrupting her, and anyway she keeps her phone off during sessions. Maybe he should get out his laptop? But he's called in sick, he doesn't want to confuse them by checking out any files. Work is not the solace for Aidan that it is for Ruth. She withdrew to it like a fucking bunker. 'I'm working,' the failsafe mantra against talking things through. Though, to be fair to her, he reminds himself, she'd needed something to succeed. On the concrete, a plane begins to taxi.

Aidan had really thought – had meant it when he promised – that they would stop at two. But the second cycle had been cancelled when there weren't any viable embryos, so of course they had kept going. And each of those times, he had put all his love into the rituals of follicles and collection and maturation and fertilisation. And each time, the same emotions. *Hope*. *Fear*. He could not have predicted that hope would be the worse of the two. Every time the phone rang with an update, he'd felt the double wave rush through his body. And watched as Ruth's face brightened, turning her beaming grin on him, or darkened, her whole body shrinking inwards.

The third cycle had been tough, Ruth's hormones like a nightmare rollercoaster. But at the end, there was a positive test, the line darker than the last time, and Ruth saying it felt different, felt right. When they went to the clinic, her hCG levels were high and continued to rise like they were meant to. The wave of hope, pure hope, was real this time. At the ten-week scan they had heard the heartbeat, fast and strong. At the twelve-week scan, they'd heard it again, and seen the blurry black-and-white shape of their future. They had started to tell people. To make lists of their favourite names. Niamh. Mia. Luke. Aidan had knelt by the bed, whispering the words over Ruth's abdomen like some kind of Merlin. Thirteen weeks of happiness.

She must have been in pain for a while before she'd told him. Aidan remembers the look of certainty on her face as he'd groped for possibilities. But it was unavoidably real when that night he'd watched her have those awful mini-contractions, seen the clots that came after, changed the towels he'd laid under her. For the last part Ruth had sat on the toilet, Aidan on a chair in the doorway. She'd caught the little thing in her hands, a tiny shrimp. All he could think to do was wrap it in tissue. The next morning, as Ruth slept, he'd taken the bundle to the hospital. He must have sat in the car for nearly an hour, unable to go in, unable to say goodbye.

Why have he and Ruth never talked about that morning? And why, afterwards, did everyone treat Aidan like he was only a spectator, even Ruth? No, that wasn't fair, he's not being fair again. Still, though, there is something in it that feels true.

The quiet in the lounge feels kind of eerie now, reinforcing the limbo inside. How unhappy is too unhappy?

The screen still says GATE IN 10 MINUTES, but Aidan picks up his case anyway. He will go down, find some relief in the terminal's noise, the distraction of other people's lives.

'It's like, going clubbing just doesn't do it for me any more, so it's hard to, like, talk to people in college who are still really into it?'

They are standing by the stall, and Jo is saying this to her friend Sam, and Sam is nodding. And though Alice has never been to a club, in fact the word 'club' doesn't even conjure any mental image beyond, maybe, a dance floor, Alice agrees.

'Yeah.'

And when Jo looks at her and smiles, Alice has to keep going.

'I used to go to parties, like, I have friends who have these parties and it's all about what you're wearing or who you're scoring, and I just –' Alice falters.

'You want to have proper conversations, yeah, about things that actually matter,' Jo says. 'Exactly. You go, girl!'

And she fist-bumps Alice, who touches her knuckles to Jo and thinks, this should be awkward, but it feels good. Only that, only touching another girl's hand, no more than that. Feel. Good.

'Is Pen okay?' Jo asks, and Alice remembers how she had just run away from Jo earlier, once she'd realised Pen was gone, and it's too big, now, to explain it. Alice feels her cheeks' sudden flush and she looks over at Pen. Pen looks okay now, she's reading a leaflet, but Alice thinks maybe she's actually taking a mini-timeout, like reading is her way of checking out a bit?

'She's fine, we just both skipped lunch,' and Jo nods at this. And it was true. Even if it wasn't the whole truth. Pen's mum had said, 'Get some food!' and then she'd said, 'Please, you and Pen have done the march, please just come home.' They had got out of the gallery and seen the burrito place, which was kind of perfect because it had been small but quiet, so it was not going to upset Pen. And it was good, actually, to eat, it made Alice feel a little more solid too. And it had been even better, when they got back to the square, to see Jo's smile suddenly flash when she saw Alice.

'I just feel like sometimes everyone talks a lot,' Jo says, and Sam nods again, 'and it's a giant cul-de-sac, we're going down it but there's nowhere to actually go.'

'Bum of the bag,' Alice says.

'Sorry?' and Jo is laughing.

'Bum-of-the-bag, that's what cul-de-sac means in, like, French.'

Jo smiles even more broadly. 'That's so cool, that you know stuff like that. Wow, I'd never even thought before of that being French?'

Alice and Pen had been walking back to her house one day and they'd seen the sign:

Cul
De
Sac

Pen had pointed to it and said 'bum-of-the-bag'. It was

kind of abrupt like Pen was sometimes, which Alice thought probably meant she was feeling shy, so she said, 'Yeah?' in a way she hoped was cool. Then Pen explained that's what the sign meant in French and how they don't even call it that in France, they say something like *voie sans issue*. Pen said that it was funny to think about how many words we use every day that are originally from another language, we never even think about them, don't even guess how many languages we are secretly speaking. Alice had looked at Pen, kind of sideways, because actually being friends with Pen was like speaking a secret language too.

'Yeah,' Alice says to Jo. 'Pen told me about it once.'

'What time are you hanging around till?' Sam asks, and it takes a moment for Alice to realise he's asking her. She glances over again at Pen.

'Um, I don't know. How about you?'

'Well, we're camping.' Sam inclines his head towards the tents slowly going up on the other side of the railings. Alice could not feel more stupid.

'Yeah, I knew that, sorry!'

'We're taking it in shifts to keep the camp secure, to have a presence,' Jo smiles. 'And, you know, to hang out with each other. I'd only met them,' she points to others slightly further off, 'online before, so this feels brilliant, you know?'

'Yeah, totally.'

'You probably have school, right, you can't stay over.'

It's not a question, just a statement of fact.

'Yeah,' Alice says, 'but I can hang out for the night. Help with the tents?' And when Jo smiles, and when Jo glances at

Sam and he raises his eyebrows at her, making Jo hide her smile but glance back at Alice, Alice knows that something is happening. Alice looks away, at the sky, the trees, the grass, the tents, the people, and thinks of Jo putting her hand on her again, of how that would feel.

4.40 pm

The table looks melancholy, littered with cake bits, and though the memory of Lisa and the baby still hovers, Ruth is alone. It is a small cast of characters, Ruth's life, but she has always told herself that she holds them tightly. Yet the baby is a month old, and this is the first she's seen of her. Ruth had had fantasies of arriving with boxed-up dinners for Lisa's fridge or freezer because Ruth was a good friend, she was one of those people who helped others. But they were just that, fantasies, and when she hadn't done those things, well, perhaps she should face the fact that she was not as generous as she'd thought.

Ruth's phone buzzes and it feels like an act of supreme muscular triumph to get this plastic object out of her pocket.

16.41 BOARDING

Ruth's thumb hovers over the screen. What to say to the husband who might be leaving you?

OKAY

Send.

In the gallery toilets, Ruth enters a cubicle, her coat brushing the seat as she turns to close the door. The hook is broken, so she puts her bag on the floor, pulls out paper and wipes the seat, for all the good it does. She sighs because it is a relief just to be in a room with a lock. Ruth undoes her belt, sits. There is a musky, almost acrid, smell from the pad. She has leaked again, perhaps when she was laughing? This is how her mother smelled and it horrifies her, the idea that this too is part of her inheritance. Ruth tenses her pelvic muscles and then allows herself to pee. She should do Kegels more often, she should start practising seriously, she is too young to be old, jesus, she doesn't even run any more for fear of wet patches (Aidan still runs, black headband, red-and-yellow runners, at least he is doing it).

She hears a flush in the next cubicle and imagines the bodies she cannot see, the row of them sitting and peeing, the water taking it away, everything behind closed doors as if that makes it clean. For all the time they spent doing it, it was not something you considered much, or only in private, what comes out of bodies. Is she definitely done? She clenches again. She really will start the exercises. Clench. Unclench. And was the paper slightly pink? What comes out of her body.

They had been pregnant. It is one of the forbidden thoughts. They had been pregnant.

It was on their third cycle, the positive test that meant they would, really would, be parents. After the false start of the first one, though, and the cancelled second, they had held off on celebrating. 'Let's make it to the first proper scan,' Aidan had said. And then, in that clinic room where she had been so many times, they had seen their baby on the screen, heard the whooshing noise of that tiny heartbeat. 'It sounds fast,' Aidan had said, but the nurse said that was normal.

It was thirteen weeks when the pains started. Snaking up her legs, so that Ruth thought it was just her veins, under pressure from all the extra blood her body was making. Then it snaked into her abdomen. And then blood. Not rusty, not old blood, a gush of bright red. And Ruth, seeing it on her fingers, had said nothing. Kept it from Aidan. Perhaps, if she did not say it, it would not be true.

The lights in the gallery toilets are not flattering, these down-lit fluorescents. Reflected in the mirror over the handbasins, Ruth looks too pale, another of her mother's bugbears. 'You look washed out,' she would say, waving a box of iron tablets. And now? Dark eyes and red patchy skin; it is hard to believe the image in the glass belongs to her.

There was no stopping it. The pain that convulsed her abdomen, that forced her to bed. Aidan had held her, and phoned the doctor, who had said she would probably pass it that day or the next. Clots had come out of her, and Ruth had wondered, is that it? But it was not really ended till late that night, hunched over the toilet, when she'd felt something leaving her, and she had reached down and caught the foetus. The silence as she held it. 'Aidan,' she'd croaked, and he had leaned gently over, seen her cradling this tiny thing in her hands. They had wrapped it in tissues, and Aidan had found a box.

The hand soap dispenser feels sticky and it drips, leaving a trail of green slime on the edge of the creamy basin. Ruth tries to concentrate on washing her hands in the lukewarm water.

She had been so angry, a wave of it like she'd never known. And maybe the purity of her anger protected her – after all, she had recovered enough to get up in the following days, to get dressed and eat and speak. To go to work. She must

144

have looked like she was okay from the outside. 'Do you feel you need to talk to someone?' the doctor had asked, looking embarrassed as he handed them a leaflet on the optional counselling service. But Ruth had been too angry to say yes.

She had waited to feel better, to feel able for it, to feel anything other than this anger. Ruth knew that miscarriages were common, was told it by doctors and nurses and, of course, by Aidan. She knew that it was something you were meant to get over. But Ruth had not. In her work, Ruth had encountered this before, this feeling, a mix of anger, numbness and blame in other kinds of victims. It didn't compute, didn't make sense, and yet in the months after the miscarriage, Ruth felt like she had been raped.

Ruth heads out of the toilets, then pauses at the mezzanine steps. She should go down, out the doors, into the world. But she is not ready for the world just yet.

BOARDING

Retrace your steps, Ruth thinks, walking back into the old building, as if it was ever possible to go back. Two cycles, they had said. Then three. And then Aidan was saying a fourth, they needed to try for a fourth time. And all the time the same question over and over in her mind: how long were you allowed to grieve, to be numb, to feel violated?

Ruth avoids the crowd and veers right, unsure of her goal. She finds herself in a small, interior room. The room is dark, the only illumination coming from the stained-glass window mounted on the wall. The colours still her, the glow of blues and greens and reds. It is a pietà in glass, as Mary holds her wasted son, the light seeming to shine from her face. The way the artist has positioned her, it's as if she is on the cross too, or maybe she is the cross, bearing a limp Jesus, his broken body sheltered by her royal-blue cloak.

Did Mary talk to God after their son's death? But then, they hadn't really shared him. What was Mary's life after? Perhaps she survived, perhaps she escaped the cycle of revenge, lived in a cottage somewhere, in the woods maybe, away from all the people who knew. She might have been self-sufficient, she might have told her own stories, served only herself. Perhaps. But all the ruined women, Ruth thinks. We can't all run away to cottages in the woods, the place would be fucking packed.

5.05 pm

'The government are just so autistic,' the guy said as he showed them how the groundsheets should be pulled flat.

He wasn't even saying it to them, he was talking to his friend, another guy, who was nodding. *So autistic*. Wouldn't it be better, Pen thinks, if they were? The climate crisis might actually get fixed.

Alice and Pen have stayed in the square to help set up tents, it's a camp, really, because it will be a whole week of protests. The people around them are laughing and having fun, the ones who are dressed up, some of them are amazing, like mermaids. Pen looks at their blue skin, at the beauty that comes out of fear.

Pen has pushed the tent peg in as far as it goes, but the ground is a bit uneven and she's not sure if she's done it right. Pen wants to ask Alice, but she's wandered over again to the next tent group. Camping is not really Pen's thing, though a garden (*hortus*) in the centre of the city is not the same as the forest places (*silva*) where Sandy takes them for walks, talking about the outdoor life as if it's something he knows anything about. It is enough to stand here, feeling pegged to the ground herself, just watching other people. Jo is moving around, smiling at everyone, she is popular, and Pen glances at Alice, who is concentrating on attaching a flag to the top of a tent. What does it mean, what do they all mean? Pen knows the answer to this question without having to think about it. It's corny and it goes against what people think of her, even her mother, but the answer is obvious: Love. You could be saved by love (not a metaphor). You could feel cold and afraid and then, because of love, someone would come to you and stand by you and rescue you. There is something else obvious, though. You could understand that it was all for love and still not understand it.

'Love is meant to be a two-way street,' Claire says, but this phrase has always puzzled Pen, because surely it means that the two people in love, on this two-way street, are travelling in opposite directions? Pen supposes it could be like her and Alice and their trains today, which is a good image. But it only works if the other person knows the plan, and they both get off at the right station so they can meet halfway. Meeting halfway is another big thing for Claire. But what if the other person is on a different street or train or journey entirely?

Alice is back, Alice is smiling and talking.

'There's a gathering,' she says. 'They're asking if we want to hang out, like, later?'

Pen doesn't understand the question for a moment, hang out with who and where? Alice's face is changing. She touches Pen's arm and looks at her in a way Pen does not want her to look. (Are you okay now?) Pen concentrates and when she glances again, Alice's face is smiling once more. Pen breathes.

'Sorry, Pen, I meant: Jo is wondering if we want to go for a drink, there's a pub they like,' Alice points north, 'that is meant to be really good and has all local drinks and stuff. What do you think? About going with Jo, and having a drink?'

Pen wishes she and Alice were back in the burrito place where it was warm and it was just the two of them and they sat on stools in the window and looked out, because that was one thing Pen could do, she could look out through glass and actually see the world as it was happening. But Alice is opening her eyes wide and looking directly at Pen, which she doesn't usually. It almost overwhelms Pen, it makes her want to close her own. She won't actually, though, because she knows that this hurts other people, will hurt Alice. So instead, she looks down at the ground.

'Yeah?' Alice asks, as if maybe Pen was nodding, not just looking away from her. 'Only if you're cool with it, though?'

Alice's voice sounds like it's happy, so Pen feels good then, at letting this plan be made without her. But when Pen looks up at Alice, her face is a little bit serious.

'I mean,' Alice says, 'we can walk with you to the station, if you want instead? The pub is, like, over the river so we'll go past the Dart, and you can go home.' Alice's voice rises at the end like it's a question.

Pen wants to say, wait a minute, so she can figure out if it was a question, or if Alice actually wants Pen to leave?

'Pen, it's fine if you want to go home.'

But it isn't fine, because they have a date later, that's what Pen wants to say. But since Alice doesn't know yet that it's a date, Pen is going to have to say something else instead.

'I don't want to go home,' Pen says, 'I mean, I have a surprise for you later.'

This is the surprise. Alice's birthday isn't until December, she's a Christmas baby. Alice hates sharing her birthday and she hates tinsel. She likes the little white lights, though, she has them up in her bedroom all year round. But she still shudders when you say 'Christmas'. So Pen has made this surprise for her, which is an early birthday present, and when she gives it to Alice, Alice will know she planned it all for her, and Alice will look at Pen, and when that happens, everything will be okay. All of which means that Pen has to go to the pub.

'Maybe the pub, though, will be too much for you. It might be loud? You might get confused or whatever again? I mean, you don't even drink.'

Pen can see that Alice's eyebrows are close together, so that means Alice is frowning. Pen is wondering if Alice drinks, or what Alice means by confused, but she has to say something.

'I have a surprise for you, for later,' Pen is just repeating herself now, unsure if this is showing grit or pleading.

'It's fine, I can get my surprise another time, I'm fine if you want to go home. Really.'

The bottom of Pen's stomach is trembling because now it feels like Alice is with her friends and Pen is the one hanging on, not like she and Alice are there together. The pub is a terrible idea, says her mother's voice, let's name the triggers, Pen. Pen doesn't want to think about triggers, she only wants to hold Alice's hand, though the memory that they have held hands today feels already uncertain.

'The surprise has to be today.'

Alice's face looks like Claire's face when she says Pen is being stubborn, being obstructive, and Pen braces her shoulders.

'So you'll come to the pub? Brilliant!' Alice smiles.

'I'll come to the pub,' Pen says.

Pen watches Alice run back, the only word she can use, run back to the group of people who are still laughing by the other tent, and is Alice actually jumping up and down, or just on her tiptoes, but still, she might jump at any moment, that is a picture of happiness. That Pen has made happen.

5.08 pm

They were not, it turned out, in it together. Every possibility Ruth had had to confess her true feelings, to say, 'I feel violated,' had passed her by, passed them both by. Ruth had feared that if she told Aidan, he would have just tried to reason her out of it. Or, worse, he would have looked at her like she was accusing him of being part of the violation. So Ruth had not told her husband the truth.

They had taken a break after the miscarriage, just a few months she'd thought at first, but it had stretched to a year. And slowly it had dawned on Ruth that she never wanted to go back. But Aidan felt differently. He did not want, was not able, to *just give up*. And Ruth could not deny him, not when there had been one remaining embryo from the third cycle. So they tried again. 'It will be a gentle cycle,' Aidan had said. On the day of the transfer, Ruth had silently cried with the pain and humiliation of it. Trousers off. Pants off. Gown on. Feet up. Knees wide. Instruments in. Aidan had held her hand. And Ruth had hated him every second. Because he was doing this to her.

Keep going, says the voice in Ruth's head, and she obeys. One foot in front of the other, into the next room. Ruth looks around at the walls. A portrait of a woman with a child on a bench looks back at her. A landscape, a man showing it all to a woman in a flowing dress. These are the kind of pictures Aidan likes, the ones in gilt frames. 'They look like real things, real people,' he would say.

Through another doorway, and there is a painting that looks like a collage, like the outline of a house, like the inside of a person. Cubist, was that the right thing to say? Ruth leans in to read the card on the wall:

Decoration by Mainie Jellett (1897–1944).
1923.

Tempera on wood panel.
Bequeathed, Evie Hone, 1955.
NGI.1326.

There is no face, no body, just shapes. Straight lines, sharp corners, curved edges, coloured dots around the edges, red yellow blue black, then larger shapes of grey and gold at the centre. Somehow an abstract painting is easier to look at, to be with. Ruth even imagines herself in it, being held within it. Ridiculous, she thinks, I am ridiculous, but it is real, this longing. She must have made a noise because the man standing beside her coughs. He is older, and he glances at her as he leans in to read the name of the painting. She had been here first, it is her painting, why should she step back. But she does, she gives way.

Ten days' wait. The unbearableness of time.

Another negative.

After the doctor's office, after the pitying looks and the soft voices and the offer of a glass of water for Aidan, who had tears pouring down his face, though no sound came out of him, after they had put their coats back on and the receptionist had said she would send on the bill, don't worry about it now, after all of that, Ruth and Aidan had stood on the street outside the clinic. People were walking and driving, living, like nothing had happened. Finally, Aidan had said, 'What do you want to do?' and she had said, 'I can't, I'm done.'

He had looked at her, his face not moving, and, too late, Ruth realised he had been asking her if she wanted a coffee, or to get a taxi home, or to go to work. She had said it too soon. Aidan had turned and started walking, up the hill, away from her. His shoulders were hunched as he trudged ahead and she followed, and she called his name a few times, but he did not respond. 'Wait,' she'd shouted, and he'd stopped short then started again once she'd caught up. And it was like that all the way home. She should have run after him, should have thrown herself at him, forced him to put his arms around her. But she had not reached out, she had not even tried to touch him. Lisa was right about that.

In front of the painting, Ruth sighs and turns away because there are no answers here. As she moves, the white-haired man speaks. 'You are enjoying it,' he says, 'I see how much you enjoy this picture. You make me want to find my favourite too.' And he smiles as he walks away.

We get each other so wrong, Ruth thinks. Perhaps in the end it was not the clinics and the jabs and the results that had broken Ruth and Aidan. It was what came after that they were no good at. In the wake of grief, they had nothing left for each other.

'Is this what you want?' Aidan had said last night, and Ruth had looked at the window, made a mirror by the night beyond, at the reflection of her body and their house and their life, and had felt disconnected from all of it. When she did not reply, the line had gone silent, she could not even hear him breathing. 'Are you there?' she had asked.

In the gift shop they don't have a postcard of the painting, so she settles for another Jellett, *A Composition*. They sell all sorts of things in the shop, not just art, not just postcards, there are jigsaws and mugs and stationery. Ruth does not want any of it, can't imagine why she is shopping, even, but the card is in her hand now, so she queues up to pay.

In the end, it wasn't what either of them wanted, was it? Aidan had needed someone to be at fault, and Ruth, not knowing what else to do, had accepted his blame. The person behind her shuffles and Ruth realises it's her turn next at the till. She holds her postcard out like an offering, so that the woman can take it from her, slot it into a paper bag. 'I'm here,' he had sighed across the phone line at last and it had been a moment of almost togetherness.

Ruth looks down through the glass top of the counter, staring at a necklace, a delicate strand of gold with small wooden cubes, pink and gold. She runs her finger across the glass, smudging it.

'Did you find everything you were looking for?' the cashier says now, and Ruth is startled. She feels like saying no, she feels like wailing it at the woman, like throwing herself on the floor and fucking howling.

'Did you find everything you were looking for?' the woman asks again as if Ruth might not have heard her the first time. And it is not a real question, it turns out, just a way of saying goodbye.

5.12 pm

'The thing is,' Jo says, 'if we only cut emissions by five per cent over ten years, we're only lowering the chances of temperatures rising by fifty per cent. It needs to be more radical. We need to imagine what a zero-emissions world would look like.' Jo's hair has fallen over her face and she twists it now, tucking it back.

Pen looks at Jo's ear, a whorl of pink skin and cartilage. Pen wonders how, if they all agree, if every person in this room agrees that this is the crisis of their generation, if the scientists agree and the governments admit they are right and it's serious and needs to be addressed and they will make-it-their-priority . . . then how is it still happening?

'The governments have to listen, they're still all just focused on the economy, economy, economy. They don't want to think about life, about the lives they're stealing. The ecosystem is collapsing now, people are dying. We're seeing floods and drought in Ireland, and we have a temperate climate – can you imagine what it's like for more extreme climates?'

Alice had said, 'It'll be easy to find a seat because it's the afternoon,' as if she did a lot of drinking-in-the-afternoon-in-pubs-in-town. Pen had nodded.

'And refugees, I mean, what we're seeing now is nothing compared to the climate refugees. There'll be wars over water. China is taking so much of the mineral deposits out of

Africa, they're shipping natural resources, and in some ways, you know, it's like slavery all over again. Plus, we're implicated. The bad guy isn't just *over there*,' Jo waves her hand around, 'the minerals go into manufacturing in China and then *we* buy all the stuff they make. The north of China is basically one giant factory, they haven't seen the sky in years, they're all wearing masks against the pollution.'

Alice had seemed excited and on edge and jittery. They had walked past the station and Pen had looked determinedly at the other side of the street, nearly saying, look, the science gallery! But Alice was in full flow about 'the guys' and Pen didn't want to look childish. And when they got there, Alice was right, it was easy to get a seat at the empty tables lined up all along one side of the pub. It was what her dad called an old-man-pub, with disapproval of course. 'Why do they not make things modern?' was one of Sandy's refrains. There are actually no old men in the bar, it's just them, and the staff look young too. But being here makes Pen know what Sandy means, it feels old-mannish.

'No one wants to admit we're at the tipping point, they all say over ten years, but we need a global effort now, climate change is generated by nations but the effects don't recognise borders, they'll be everywhere. We need a coordinated lockdown of emissions, because it's unprecedented, what we're facing. We need to make it real to people.'

When it had got bad a few years ago, before the word autism was ever used, before Pen knew for sure that she was not broken, she had asked Claire what she'd change, if she could change one thing about Pen. Pen had been hitting her palm against her own chest, standing facing the wall, because these were the only ways she knew how to feel she was real.

'What,' she had gasped out between beats, 'what would you change? Tell me.'

'Pen, please stop hitting yourself so we can talk.'

'What – would – you – change!'

And so Claire had told her.

'Other people.'

That's all Claire had said she would change, and something about those two words had given Pen a kind of calm, had slowed the beats of her hand, had allowed her to breathe again.

Sola. That is the Latin for 'solitary'. Which is the feeling you get when you realise, or when you let yourself know, that the world is made for other people. *Sola.* It was true that other people said, 'Oh, sorry,' when they saw you stumble and fall. But they did not care, not really, or not enough to change. Because they are, deep down, or not even that deep, pleased and happy and reassured that the world is made for them.

Pen takes some of her drink and thinks maybe it will help the words to flow. She is drinking blackcurrant because she doesn't drink alcohol (which is what people mean when they say 'drink'). Pen hates the way 'drink' makes people act stupidly, though that is what other people seem to like. She doesn't like the way Claire laughs so much when she's had too much wine. Apparently, Alice does 'drink', so she had ordered a pint of cider and it is there, on the table, next to Pen's narrow glass, which looks like a child's drink.

Pen should be at home. Soraya will be home by now, doing

her homework at the kitchen table, or watching TV, or in her room doing whatever she does behind the '*Keep Out: Private*' sign. It is hard to believe that other things are going on elsewhere still, life as usual, life to a timetable, without any connection to this moment, this feeling. Pen balances on a stool with wooden legs and a kind of soft velvet cushion. All the stools are different styles. Alice is on the one next to her, which has a leather seat and metal legs. Jo is on the bench against the wall, facing down the table like a preacher.

'Technical solutions, they keep going on about technology will solve this, technology is driving this too, let's admit that, that thing in your hand, it's not a phone, it's a grenade that is constantly exploding our carbon budget. We need to get to zero emissions. It sounds impossible, they all say we're crazy, but that's the science, scientists are looking at the air, at the melting permafrost, at the continued exploitation of fossil fuels. We still burn turf in this country, for god's sake.'

'For peat's sake,' someone says, to a chorus of groans. Pen looks towards him, but she doesn't know his name. She thinks of the other kind of day she had imagined, with her and Alice and the city around them, and the way they would understand each other. She wonders if it is still possible. What did you want from another person, was it the same or bigger than what you wanted from yourself?

'Yeah, peat, thanks, peat sucks in CO_2 but we're burning it, releasing thousands of years of gases. We need leadership, for the world to recognise the real danger of this, not buying up carbon budgets of other countries, just moving emissions overseas, basically, we can't close our eyes to the crisis, it's taking hold, infecting us like a virus, the scale of death is enormous. In Sudan it's epic, the Sahara Desert is getting, like, way bigger every year and so many people have died in Darfur, and, y'know, been displaced.'

Pen could touch Alice so easily.

'If that was white people dying, the world might notice or do something. Africa is the lowest emitter of carbon, but the most affected, it's climate *in*justice. Climate injustice is what we should be talking about.'

Everybody murmurs and smiles tight smiles, no teeth showing, no squeezed-happy eyes. Jo takes a big mouthful of beer. Pen will wait for someone else to start talking and then she will lay her arm on the table next to Alice's, will lift her little finger, will touch the side of Alice's hand. Touch.

But it is Alice who starts to speak.

'Because climate change is not really being taught in schools, I mean, we'll be the ones who have to live in this world, but it's not even on the curriculum, we've got no, no ecological literacy, I mean, we barely even recycle at our school. Nothing's happening.'

Pen thinks of the student committee on climate change, she thinks of the school strike, she thinks of the civics class last year on global health – weren't they all signs of something happening? Loyally, though, Pen nods.

Alice looks at Jo, Jo smiles at her, and they each bend their heads towards the other. And Pen thinks of all the things that will be lost.

'Four hundred billion,' Pen says. Eyes look at her. 'Four hundred billion tonnes of ice lost from Greenland.'

Her voice sounds like her voice.

'Ninety-three per cent, the sea absorbs ninety-three per cent of the extra heat created by greenhouse gases. Sixty per cent of coral reefs will be critically threatened in the next ten years. Twenty-six per cent of the CO_2 we produce is absorbed by oceans at a rate of twenty-two million tonnes per day, leading to a thirty per cent increase in ocean acidity.'

Pen's fingers are bouncing off her thigh, stim, stim, stim. But this is easy, a piece of cake, and the words flow because facts are her friends. Pen feels Alice's eyes on her and it almost burns her skin.

'Temperatures are already above freezing in the Arctic, they will rise to five degrees Celsius by 2050 at the latest. 2016 had the lowest sea-ice extent on record, but this will become common, and Greenland could be ice-free by 2050, leading to chain-reaction melting, raising global sea levels by two to eight feet. Displacing four million people. Up to seven hundred million climate refugees by the same year, 2050.'

There is a pause. Pen's blood is coursing inside her because everyone has listened, they have been quiet and kept still, even people who were talking while Jo was speaking, and this is what it feels like to have people interested in you and respectful of you and to have people like you. This feeling. Alice is beaming at her, looking around to the others, saying, 'She's really good with numbers,' as if Pen is something she owns.

Jo's face is more serious, though her eyes are crinkled, which means kind. Jo says, 'See, that's brilliant, these are the facts we need. Wow, Pen, we should get you up onstage, you've such a serious way of talking, people would listen to you.'

Pen shakes her head, she didn't even know she was going to speak, she's still pumping with adrenaline that she has. Jo is smiling properly now, and the others begin to talk again, talking about a new Ireland or a new world or the old world, it is all the same to Pen right now. The guy who said the thing about peat gets up and leans over to Jo, 'Another?' he says, and Jo nods, holding up her glass to him, 'Cheers.' Then she turns back to Pen. 'Your mum's such a great lecturer, it obviously runs in the family.'

'What did you study with her?' Pen has asked a normal kind of question.

'Victorian poetry, oh wow, I loved it, all "If you sit down at set of sun"', amazing, you can tell she loves it.'

Without thinking about it, Pen recites, ' "Morning and Evening / Maids heard the goblins cry".' Alice watches. Alice is wrong, it's not numbers, it's memory Pen is good at.

' "Goblin Market"! Yes! Or Barrett Browning: "I love thee with the breath, / Smiles, tears, of all my life". Whoosh!'

And Pen continues, ' "I . . . Will write my story for my better self, / As when you paint your portrait for a friend, / Who keeps it in a drawer and looks at it / Long after he has ceased to love you, just / To hold together what he was and is." '

No one else pays attention as the lines ring in the air. There's a conversation further down the table about sea levels, about climate deniers, about white flight, but here, where they are, it's only Pen and Alice and Jo, and Pen is at the centre.

'That's amazing,' Alice says, 'I didn't know you did that, said poetry.' And Pen, who has been trying to find a way to talk to Alice for so long now, is amazed again at how someone else's words can be hers.

'She's political, Barrett Browning, that's what Dr—I mean, your mum taught me, there's a poem about children weeping in the country of the free, that would actually work for a rally now, because that's what we're doing, we need maybe a poet laureate for the climate.'

Pen likes the cadence of a line, the way you can understand

the rhythm first, before you understand the words. She likes how the rhythm tells you what the poet was feeling, tells you what to feel.

'Hey, folks,' Jo raises her voice, 'Pen's given me this idea,' a smiling glance at Pen, 'for an Irish poet laureate of climate.' Instantly someone is talking about non-hierarchies, pulling Jo in, who smiles again at Pen. 'Not a hierarchy, a voice for all of us.'

Pen keeps looking at Alice, hoping that the thing that got broken earlier during Pen's episode is fixed, is being fixed. Alice is looking down into her drink and then back up at the room, along the tables. Her leg is approximately five centimetres away from Pen's. All it would take, such a slight gesture, is a tiny move to the right.

Pen looks above Jo's head and sees a corner of sky through the window, cut off at the bottom by the edge of the bench, and at the top by a mini-blackboard listing all the local beers Alice had wanted.

Pen's leg swings four centimetres to the right.

Then one more centimetre.

Alice looks round, almost directly at Pen. And Pen does not imagine it. There is a slight pressure, as Alice's leg presses back against Pen's.

The world is made still and beautiful with love.

Sanctus.

5.58 pm

The flight attendant walks down the aisle asking about duty free and telling them to, 'Press your call bell if you want to make a purchase.' At least Aidan got the window seat, though it means his knees are jammed against the seat in front, the price of the wider horizon. He looks down at the flickering lights, checks the flight path. They're over north Wales. He looks again at the magazine, some of its pages torn as if a previous passenger had wanted to keep the tips on visiting Haarlem or Munich to themselves. Ruth did that sometimes, amassing a folder at home of all these places and things to do in the future, a list that could never be accomplished. 'What's the point?' he'd say, but she'd only shrug and tell him he'd be glad of them one day.

Aidan glances over at the man in the aisle seat. He's barely moved all flight, barely even looked up, glued to his screen. The seat between them is empty and at least there's that, a bit of extra room. Aidan is grateful, really, for the silence. He wonders will they do the awkward dance at the end, jostling to see who is the most efficient at getting their jacket, their luggage down from the overhead locker. He wonders if the man, if anyone, can tell just by looking at him that he is still lost.

'We can do this. Please, Ruth, just look at me.'

In the supermarket car park a year ago, the boot full of groceries, they had both seen the family of five opposite, children unloading one after another from the back seat of an estate car. Had counted them, one two three. Aidan saw Ruth's shoulders dip, wanted to say that he knew, that it wasn't fair, but it wouldn't have made either of them feel any better.

'Aidan, I'm so tired.'

'I know.' He had paused, risked trying to change the tone. 'We can take a holiday, to Wexford, or to Spain, maybe? A break would be good.'

'You're only saying that because you think it gives us a better shot.'

'I'm saying it because we both need a break. Go for walks, get a bit of heat, get away from all this. Nice dinners, tapas maybe.'

'But no wine with dinner, right?'

'No wine won't kill us, Ruth.'

'I would just like there to be some time to be me. To be us.'

'That's what I'm saying. We can be.'

The parents were swinging the youngest child between them, the older two driving the trolley. Aidan watched as they rounded the corner, out of sight. He began again.

'You've been working so hard, Ruth, you can't burn the candle at both ends. It's not wrong to need a break. And when we're a bit restored, yeah, we'll have a better shot.'

'What if it doesn't work again, Aidan? What if there's another miscarriage or just another failed cycle? I can't take that.'

'This could be the time, Ruth. This could be the one.' It was such an automatic line. 'One is all we need.'

'I'm sick of it, Aidan. We've tried four times.'

'Ruth,' Aidan had kept his voice level, 'I think we could be successful if we try again.'

'And if we aren't?' Ruth's chin almost rested on the steering wheel. 'If we aren't, Aidan? What do we do then?'

At least, at that stage, she was still talking about it. He'd let himself believe it was only another hiatus. In idle moments, Aidan had even composed imaginary forum posts: BFP! The break was all we needed! or Long journey, but it was all worth it! He couldn't bear to articulate the real version: Have to beg my wife yet again to do another cycle. Feel like we might never get there. How long was it before he knew there would be no fifth cycle? Not a hiatus, but the end.

Below, the country comes into view, the Dublin coastline, the jutting hump of Howth, a lighthouse blinking at the far end of the bay. There is a grinding sound, which must be the wheels descending. The press of gravity keeps them held steady in their seats, resisting the pull to the left as the plane wheels around. The man in the aisle seat rests his hand on his bag to stop it sliding off the empty middle chair, though the flight attendant had asked him to put it under the seat in front. They're close to the ground now, and there is a strange moment as the plane seems to slow and then to accelerate, controlled no doubt by a pilot but feeling like something going wrong. The flaps on the wings go up, slowing the plane as the wheels hit, then bounce, then make full contact with the ground.

Aidan thinks of how much he has loved Ruth, how much he loves her even now. He thinks of everything he will lose. If he is honest, he does not blame her for needing to stop, but that doesn't stop him being angry at her. It is too hard to feel the life, the love he wanted, be dismissed by the person who was meant to share it with him.

6.01 pm

Alice and Pen are standing outside the pub. The bells of the Angelus are still echoing. Alice had looked a bit surprised when Pen suggested they could talk outside, but then as Pen stood up, she followed.

'Are you okay?' Alice says.

Pen shakes her head, not to say no, but to dislodge the earlier bit when she wasn't okay, to separate then from now. If Alice was really looking at her, she would see Pen is new now.

'I got you something for your birthday, an early birthday thing,' Pen begins, concentrating on looking at the seam of Alice's jacket shoulder. 'A surprise.'

'Wow, I had no idea,' Alice says. Her voice sounds a bit quiet, but her face is not doing anything bad.

'A concert ticket. I got me – I got us – two concert tickets. For tonight.'

'Wow,' Alice says again, but she's sort of smiling? 'I mean, what concert?'

'So, you know the way you love Florence?'

'But she's not on tour—'

'No, but this group, one of the members of Florence plays with them, with her, and they're, like, inspired by Arctic exploring, and they have a whole orchestra. They raise money for Greenpeace.' Pen risks a glance. Alice looks like her face is making up its mind how to look. 'They're like a blend of chamber music and jazz.'

Alice's face is still not decided.

'It's hard to explain, they're really, really good. I got us two tickets. It's the National Concert Hall so there's seats and it won't be dark so we'll be safe, and we can get something to eat if we go, on the way, there's a vegetarian place. I have it marked on my places on the map.'

And Pen breathes and says the scary thing. 'It will be,' she glances at Alice, 'it will be a date.'

Pen wants to tell Alice how she had watched the group do a tiny-desk-concert online, which was cool, and how she liked the way they talked about what they did, and the sound they made. How they made her want to know about music. It was all about counting, but counting in a way that made it look like you weren't. She wants to say, *Ricercar*. The word sounds good in Pen's mouth, and she is just about—

'What?' Alice says.

Pen has dried up. She can't explain that *Ricercar* is a Renaissance musical fugue form, those words won't come out, and she just has '*Ricercar*' going round and round in her mouth and mind and ear and heart because she and Alice are like a human fugue and she wants to say that to her, about the fugue being like a kind of love, because Alice plays piano so she should understand, but she doesn't say it because Alice's face has turned away.

Alice is not looking at Pen or at the street or the trees across the road or up at the sky trying to figure out what time it is from the light left, or, even, is Alice breathing? And then she speaks.

'I'm sorry, I'm sorry, Pen, I thought we were just good friends. I don't, I don't want that. It's not you, it's me, I'm—'

Are Alice's eyes wet? Because they are shining, and now she is looking at Pen, staring at her and not speaking again but the look is harder and more painful. Pen reads it. Far too much. Not enough. Nothing.

'The concert is tonight,' Pen's voice sounds altered, as if it could not be emitting from her chest, her throat. Alice, her best friend, her only person, who has lain on her bed next to her, who has breathed in and out with her, who has touched her—

'I can't,' Alice says, and backs away.

Pen has never been hit. Not even when Claire says she's beyond-the-limit-Pen, or driving-me-mad-Pen, or I-just-need-to-take-a-five-minute-break-Pen. No one has ever hit her, though maybe come close, but this is what it must feel like to be hit in the chest, across all your body, because Pen is not moving but she is also travelling through space and time, propelled by a blow to her solar plexus. And there is not enough oxygen in this Real Life world.

Alice said no. Pen had not planned for this, she had thought maybe Alice would ask questions or she would want to hug Pen or something else would happen, but that something would be not this. Alice said no. Actually, Alice didn't even say no, she said—

No air.

Breathe anyway.

It is like she hears the woman's voice from earlier. In and out. And Pen tries to follow the instruction, though she can't shut her eyes because then she'll lose her balance, so instead she looks at the pavement, at the place where Alice was standing, and she whispers, In, and then Out, and somehow the breath is coming in and out of her body.

Pen feels a shiver, is this cold she feels, or else she's just shaking. Pen's jacket and backpack are on her stool, she'd left them on the stool next to Alice and across from Jo, next to a person whose name she didn't know, maybe he'd been called Sam, she didn't know, it's not a problem, her bag is safe, but moving her feet, that's a problem. The window is right there and she can see the table next to theirs but the sign for stupid beers is hiding her table. Their table. Hiding.

Pen is no longer on the street. Pen is standing over her stool, no idea how she got here, how is this where she is? But Alice is not on her stool. Pen's jacket and backpack are there. Alice's jacket is there. Jo is talking to maybe-Sam.

'Where is Alice?' Pen is using her loud voice.

'Sorry? Oh, I thought outside with you?' Jo says.

'No, no, she came in,' says maybe-Sam, pointing to the back. 'Loo?'

Pen keeps standing there and she can see Jo's face moving and her mouth is moving but it's like there is a loud buzzing in Pen's head and she can't hear the words. The name for what Jo's face is doing is 'worried' but that word seems to come from really far away, and Pen just thinks, In and Out, and hopes that the dizzy feeling will go away, because what is worse than Alice saying no, or Alice not being here, is Alice seeing her fall over and having to call Pen's mum and having to fix Pen, and it will be like being back in the wardrobe and how when the door was finally opened Pen crawled out like an animal, making groaning noises, and everyone backed away from her.

There is Alice's face, above the others, Jo points. Alice is moving towards her, she is looking at Pen's face. And she touches Pen. Alice touches Pen as she sits down, but not in a

deliberate way, in an ignoring way, the way your body sometimes touches a stranger's because they are standing in your
way, and Pen is not sure if she or Alice is the one who flinches
most. 'Oh,' Alice says, 'your phone went.' Her shoulder is
side-on to Pen, her face pointing towards Jo, Pen can't read
it, but she reads it.

'Alice.'

It is a whisper.

'Alice.'

'Have a good time at the concert, Pen. The box office
might take the extra ticket back.'

'Oh, what concert?' asks Jo, then slides her eyes away at
Alice and Pen's silence, which means they are still sharing
something, even if that thing is not talking.

Pen steps back.

People might be looking, but she does not care if they do,
that's not on the list of things to care about any more.

6.20 pm

The gallery is closing. Ruth is still by the door, unsure of where to go. Home? Not yet. She sees the windows lit up across the street.

Inside the pub it's quiet, still early, though there's a group with the tables pulled together, laughing, and soon they will be loud, they have that air about them. The young man behind the bar nods to her and she goes up to order.

'A dry day they got anyway,' says the barman as he takes up a glass, but Ruth looks blank. 'For the protests,' he says, nodding at the TV screen and its carnival of protestors waving signs and banners. 'We get a lot of students in here, they're keen. Doing no harm, that's what I say.' Ruth barely smiles in acknowledgement, and the barman knows she's another one of those, they come for somewhere to be. He won't bother her by asking what kind of gin she prefers, goes for the Dingle, safe bet.

'Take a seat,' he says, 'I'll drop it over to you.'

The glass leaves a wet mark on the beer mat, Ruth swirls it to hear the ice rattle. She nurses the drink, staring at nothing. Is this what you want, he had said, but he was not really asking, it was not a plea or a request. He was avoiding saying that it was not what he wanted.

A cheer goes up from the group by the door as more come to join them, and it is surprising to see them in such full swing – a Monday night – perhaps it is a work leaving do, perhaps a reunion. The barman goes over to them, what would they like, holding his hands wide, earning his tips.

Aidan had said she was not easy, but wasn't that another avoidance tactic? A cover-up for his real point, that without children, she is not enough.

Her pocket buzzes and, though Ruth has the urge to ignore it, she takes it out. A missed message.

LANDED

Ruth hadn't heard the bleeps, or, no, that was it, the phone was still on silent from the gallery.

So, he is coming home.

What does it even mean? Enough. 'Stop! Enough,' her mother would shout, meaning it was over. Ruth clinks the ice in her glass again, raises it in an ironic toast, trying to pretend she is not a woman in a bar raking through the entrails of her marriage. How had she not seen this coming? How did she get Aidan so wrong? So much for being an analyst.

She will tell him of the affair, that will seal it, and he will leave her for sure then. Or maybe she will be the one to move out. Ruth imagines saying this to him, 'I'll move out,' imagines the look of acceptance on Aidan's face. At least, that way, she will have some control. *I am the captain of my fate.* Was that the line? What a fucking joke! Another sip. Perhaps she will just stay here instead, get slowly drunk.

She will move out, okay, make yourself imagine what comes next, Ruth. She'll have to get a flat for herself, maybe somewhere nearer work. She's always wanted to live near a park, perhaps the Phoenix Park, then. She'll go back to running, or long walks, she could probably even do yoga in the park. But then they will have to sell the house. That does not feel like an easy thing to imagine. All the things that go with that decision. Will she need a new solicitor? A new will? And they will have to split their possessions. Ruth should start mentally tagging things now, yours and mine, hers and his. *Don't, Ruth. You know how dangerous it is to imagine something into being.*

It would be easier if they had less to lose. Ruth can remember, and it is not so long ago really, how Aidan would clear his throat so that she would look up from what she was doing, and he would just smile at her, and she would smile back. 'Boo!' he'd say, and she'd laugh at the ridiculous word, laugh because they were so happy. And they could not get enough of talking, late into the night sometimes, talking like this was the most important thing in the world, hearing the other person's words. It was a drought now, oh god, a drought of words and gestures and love, but it had been *radiant* once. How had they thrown away this precious thing?

Maybe they had been too happy. They had sex like breathing, not just at the start, but for years. With a kind of pure joy at being wholly themselves with one another. After sex, Aidan would get sleepy, his relaxed face defenceless. Ruth would wait a while, knees pressed to her chest, then when it was safe to move, she would go to the bathroom to pee, seeing her flushed face in the mirror and smiling. I am here, I am desired. Ruth would come back into the bedroom slowly, allowing the scene to reveal itself. And with hands still a little wet, she would trace a line from his toe to his lips, watching his face twitch with anticipation. It seems so far away.

The phone buzzes on the table and, as if moving through water, she presses the button to see the screen.

IN A TAXI

Ruth sips her drink, pretending a calm she does not feel. What if it really is lost?

Run!

Stay!

She thinks of her first day, three years ago, the first day of clients in the new practice. It was after the second cancelled cycle, when the numb fear had started, the fear that she could not have children. Ruth remembers how nervous she was that morning, how she'd got to the office early, fresh coffee, flowers (unscented) and the softest brand of tissues. How she'd sat, waiting for this other part of her life to begin. Twenty minutes before the client appointment her phone had buzzed and she'd chastised herself for not turning it off, but it was a message from Aidan: Look in your pencil case. She had thought it was a joke at her expense, because he teased her for carrying a pencil case like she was still in school. But she had unzipped it and seen the yellow note and unfolded it. '*I believe in you.*' That was all it said. What would she trade, oh, not for a baby, but to have that back.

Her phone buzzes again and she presses the button to light up the screen.

SEE YOU AT HOME?

It is the question mark that does it. Something as little as that deciding your fate. Ruth moves before she knows it herself, almost knocking the table, the chair giving a screech, the door of the pub banging behind her, the colder air outside a shock. The canal will be jam-packed at this time, she thinks, better to head for Cuffe Street, hail one there.

As Ruth overtakes a group of shoppers, she imagines Aidan in the back of the taxi, his thumb hovering over the screen. He would be saying no to the port tunnel, he'll risk Drumcondra, looking out at the roads, and Dublin is not the prettiest when approached from the airport, but maybe he had seen the curve of Dublin Bay as the plane flew over. Ruth crosses at the lights at the bottom of Dawson Street, retracing her route, past the empty space behind its palisades, and was that only today? It feels a lifetime away. Perhaps Aidan had realised his texts were – what? – too gruff, too peremptory, too like a test? And now, as he travels back towards their life, he is thinking of her.

Ruth hates the people in her way, as she rounds the Green. Let the traffic be unexpectedly quiet, she wills, let me get there before him, let me be the home he is coming to. Her breath is ragged now but she's past the Unitarian and here's the corner, and if there is a god there will be an empty taxi. She holds her hand out, and one swerves to the kerb. Ruth gets into this stranger's car and gives her address. As they take off, she remembers the book she didn't collect, but it does not matter.

Had she really thought she would leave him? Or that she would let him leave her? Past the technology institute and the cathedral spire, a hard left, red brake lights stretching out ahead. Had she really thought – only this morning – that perhaps this was for the best, that it was not what she wanted, that there was nothing left to catch hold of and say, no, this is mine? But now. It is as if the love has come back into her body.

They go through more lights, the road climbing slightly, and Ruth looks again at her phone, at the text, at the question mark, and it feels like the first real question he has asked her in, oh, in years. Asking her if she will be there.

It is a thing, as they come up to Leonard's Corner and the

bridge ahead, the same bridge from this morning but it is different now because now she is going home. It is a thing, Ruth thinks, that if you forced yourself to feel the pain then you could also feel the joy. She will say this to Aidan and he will look doubtful, but she will mean it and maybe her meaning it will make both of them believe. Ruth leans forward to tell the driver to bear left of the park, to head for the Five Points.

The car sails into the square, through the gap left by the cars parked on either side, over the first set of speed bumps, then turns left. 'Just here,' she says to the driver, and he nods to her in the mirror. The car pulls up and Ruth has a last-minute wave of fear, of doubt, gazing out the taxi window at the house. The light is on. He is here before her and she is coming home to him, but how, really, can she come home at all? (One night Aidan had said, 'I can't imagine a life without children.' And she had said, 'I can.')

She won't get out of the car, she'll ask the driver to go on, to take her somewhere else, but she's paying the fare now, and pushing the gate, and the hinges creak and Ruth thinks, oh, he'll hear that, and she's nearly at the porch now, finding her key, and she can see him through the front window, standing in the middle of the living room, looking around him. She's shutting the front door, the house giving a shudder of recognition, and she's coming into the room, and he is looking at her, and she wants to hold him because his face is so open and so sad and so lost. And she almost laughs, the way you do when you're really afraid, because here is the storm at last.

Ruth stands facing Aidan, looking at his face. Not laughing, serious now. Because there is the thought. There is the thing she has not allowed. There it is.

He has stopped loving her.

6.20 pm

She does not love you back. She does not love you back and all the things that means for how you feel and how you are and even who you are. Alice does not love you back and it is like black curtains at the side of everything and you can only exist between them, and the space is getting narrower and narrower, and there is the buzzing noise still in your head. You might faint.

You can walk without seeing, you can walk on a street with tears rolling down your face without being seen. You can walk past a building that you know somehow is the pro-cathedral, and only notice it because of the sleeping bags on the steps. You can be a body in space, and time is collapsing, but no one will see, only you can see, and you can't see because there are tears filling your eyes and on your cheeks and dripping off your chin and salty in your mouth.

You begin to see again only when you reach a junction and hear a horn go and realise you have stepped off the pavement and onto the tarmacadam of the road and the mirror on the side of the car has almost touched you. And it is like a thing happening to your body and suddenly you notice you are on a street and you notice all the other bodies, all the lives, all the people walking with a purpose invisible to you, but unmistakably there. They are going somewhere, coming from somewhere, going to be with someone. Women carry bags, they walk lopsided, men bounce more, hands in their pockets. The children are in a different world, hurry up slow down stop doing that. They wear clothes, different colours, mainly black or grey, they are important but also somehow ordinary.

You notice everyone has a phone, they are talking or listening or holding, looking, monitoring, all of them, armoured. Women with faces like masks, men with caps and slouches, that's the young ones, then there's a divide, an edge, and you see it, you've never seen it before but you see young people and old people, where are the people in-between, the people not in shoes with sloping worn-out soles, without shopping bags, you search for a face, a back you recognise, you see no one, but they see you. A group of girls outside a shop and they are bright, they are loud, they are happy. Under the bridge for Connolly train station and maybe you could get on a train and go home? Or maybe you could go somewhere else, to the south end perhaps, to stand on the stony beach and look out at the sea, the acidifying rising sea. Or go north, follow its line the few stops to her house, sit in Fairview Park where you both had a picnic once, sit and watch and wait. Only that would make you afraid, under the trees, and maybe she would come home by another way. Instead you could stay on the train and go further, get off at Howth, or further yet over the bridge that nearly collapsed and see the sea there instead, it is always the sea you want to see. But then, you would still be alone, so you turn away from the station's tower, and now you are on streets you don't know, turning by instinct but your instinct must be all wrong because you-are-so-autistic and she said no and she looked at you like—

You walk past more girls hanging on railings and they call out to you but you're elsewhere, there's a child's mini-buggy in the middle of the pavement, so you walk around it and there aren't really cars on this street, you notice that and you notice the mix of old and new buildings and the old ones are nicer, and how can you be heartbroken and still noticing things like this? The world is meant to dissolve or be over and you should be blind because you can't see her any more because she looked at you like—

There is a playground on this street with trees, and nature is still there, though it's boxed in and fenced in and only allowed in rectangles, and someone has a scooter on the pavement and you don't move as he scoots towards you and he's in a black jumper and black jeans and you have time to notice his eyes are blue, sort of, and his elbow hits your arm and you stop walking, and there is a lady then who touches you on the shoulder and says, 'Are you alright,' and you don't say anything but your face is still wet, and the lady says to the man beside her, 'I think she's not all there,' so you say, 'Sorry,' and your voice still works and then you say, 'Thank you,' because she was nice, and you keep walking.

There is a sign: N1, N2 and ✈

The building on the corner has big windows covered with ads for the kind of shop that could be there and now you can get your laundry and an ironing service, years of experience and Hill 16 pub, what does that mean? It's uphill is what it is. The old buildings are back now, plain and tall, and there are more trees in another square, all the trees in the city.

You see a spire and you could turn right, you could go straight, but somehow your body turns left towards the stone spire, and you see signs for B&Bs and maybe you were here once with your mother to see a play in a small room where you had to stand watching an older man crying because the younger man couldn't love him. And afterwards Clàire had bought you an ice-cream and you had eaten it, first breaking off the chocolate in shards and then licking the creamy inside bit, the actual ice-cream.

There is a yellow-and-green-mosaic shop on the corner selling news, and a closed-up shop called Tip Top Cakeshop, and you look up at the street signs and the streets are called great, which sometimes means pregnant and sometimes means in love. *I was great with her.* But she looked at you like—

The church ahead of you has scaffolding and then there is another square with more trees, and you know from a school trip that it is the Garden of Remembrance, and you don't know how a garden can remember. And beyond you see the gallery that you visited too, with the LED installation outside of a walking lady, always moving, always lit up, and you are like her, walking walking, and you are not like her because she does not feel anything, she is only a machine.

The gates of the square are closed and there are a few men standing around, there is a bag on the ground between their feet and they are drinking out of cans, and you look at them as you wait for the lights to change. Inside the railings you can see the pool that reaches to the end and there are steps and then twisting metal figures who are the children that were cursed into being swans. You know that feeling, of being trapped, of the outside not matching the inside, of needing something that will come from outside to set you free.

It is getting darker.

Maybe she is in the pub, and maybe she's with Jo, and maybe she's with the guy whose name does not exist. So you go downhill and there are lots of people because finally you are at O'Connell Street, so you walk under the square trees and past pillars and spires. You feel hungry and you stop at the counter, a booth really, because it smells good. The girl in the hairnet fries hot batter for you and dips it in sugar and you take the bag and it's hot and sweet and crunchy and you shouldn't eat food like this because blood-sugar-levels, but you need this because fuck the rules right now because she looked at you like—

Why did she?

You get to the river again and you stand on the bridge and you look towards the sea you can't see. There's a new bridge which Claire showed you because it is named after-a-woman-at-last. But the only thing you think is that you could turn here and go back. You could turn and walk and retrace and resay, or say sorry or say other things you don't mean, or stand or sit and feel small, there are so many ways to feel small. You could do these things and maybe she would like you again. Maybe. Maybe it would be enough just to sit near her. But you look at the lights on the water and the lights on the ugly tower that-isn't-ugly because it has pretty lights on it now, and who cares about carbon when this is so pretty, and you look at the railway bridge and the old Custom House beyond and the tram tracks in front of you. And somehow all these things mean you do not want to go back.

Heart of stone Heart of a lion Heart of gold Heart's desire Heart and soul let your Heart rule your head pour out your Heart to somebody wear your Heart on your sleeve set your Heart on something speak from the Heart win someone's Heart have a big Heart the Heart of the city a broken Heart.

You know that the pain in your chest is because you are tired and not breathing deeply enough. You know that the heaviness of your body is because you have had sugar and you are tired and you are not breathing deeply enough. You know that you feel lost because you are not following your plan and plans are what make you feel safe. But you also know that the pain in your chest and the heaviness and the lostness are because you have a broken heart and sometimes the metaphor is real.

People are walking – going going going.

So you may as well go too.

You take your broken heart filled with sugar and you cross at the lights and the cars and the people and you go out in front of them all and you go around the front of Trinity, and you follow the tram tracks and you notice the hole where the building used to be, with the cranes lit up, and your legs are complaining because being heartbroken is exhausting and you are ready-to-drop but you keep walking, past the bookshop and the Hibernian Way and the mayor's house until you get to the top, until you are standing facing Stephen's Green. There is no vision like earlier, no bleached or poisoned trees. The park is closed. So you cross the tracks and you walk around it and the sugar is keeping your veins alive and you don't know, really, what level feels like anyway so, head spinning, you walk between the cars and along the railings till you reach the far edge where you cross again. The sign on the wall says Earlsfort Terrace.

You look ahead and keep walking, trying not to stumble, and then you see the stone swags of the gates and the lights of the concert hall are on.

They're on for you. Which is a thought you could not have imagined having after she looked at you like—

And your phone is buzzing. How many times now?

Pull it out to look at the screen even though that feels like hope and despair all at once.

Where are you?
Where are you?
Where are you?

Here.

And you know that you should reply, because Claire is worried, because Claire is your champion. But you also know that you are doing the thing you need to do and she would not understand because she does not think of you as someone who can be in love and that is sad and true and lonely but you will not give it up, this love, not even when she looked at you like—

And you go up the steps and a man opens the door for you, for you, and it's bright but there aren't many people so you're okay, and you see a sign for tickets and you cross the red expanse between the white pillars and you say your name at the lighted window and they give you a brown envelope and it has 'p.o'neill' on it and you open the envelope and the woman at the counter points and you go through doors and see chandeliers and more doors where a woman checks your ticket and asks if you have a guest and you say no, which nearly rips your guts out, but you're in now and you find the M and the 17 and it's your seat or you could sit in 18 too, but you look at it and think, that's where she would have sat. Except she said no and looked at you like—

7.45 pm

The quiet of the house had been soothing, grounding, and Aidan had breathed it in, thinking that it was good to come home, to the smell and feel of your own place. There was something solid about the fireplace and the mantel and the furniture, something unchanged and unchanging, something that told him he belongs here. He was relieved to be alone. When he heard the gate creak, the sound of Ruth's key in the door, he had not moved to greet her. In the pause before she came through the living-room door, he willed her to change her mind, to go upstairs first or back the way she'd come. Let me have this, he silently wished.

But no, Ruth is standing in the room with him now, disturbing this space, and he feels the rush of irritation, again, for the way she always insists on a reaction, to be heard and seen at exactly the moment that she wants, irrespective of where you are or what you are feeling.

Aidan finally looks around at his wife. Ruth's face is flushed, she holds her keys as if hoping they will open something further.

'I wanted to be home, to welcome you home,' she says.

'I didn't expect that.'

'I missed you,' she says.

Aidan lets that one hang because he is not ready, because it is too early to claim that he did not miss her.

'How was your flight?' she asks.

'Usual,' and Aidan wonders why she can't see he does not want to talk, that he needs the quiet. 'I went through the new terminal. No sign of Brexit, yet. It's all they can talk of, though, over there, the advertising industry doesn't know whether to stick Union Jacks on every label or leave them off entirely. You get this sense no one is saying what they really feel either. You never know what the other person voted,' Aidan says, shrugging.

'And London? Your weekend?'

'It was good.' Don't say anything else, he tells himself, don't talk just because you're nervous, because someone needs to fill the space. Don't tell her about drinks on Friday night, the hangover of Saturday. Don't tell her about the room service. Don't tell her about today's walking, all the hours of his weekend filled with self-loathing. Don't tell her any of it.

A tiny frown between her brows. 'Good, great,' she says.

'It was nice,' Aidan says, 'to only have myself to think of.'

Ruth's turn to shrug. She takes off her jacket, and he has a flash of seeing her, just as she turns to hang it on a chair, of seeing her as a stranger. Intimidating. She walks across the room, opens the door and goes out. Almost involuntarily, Aidan follows her down the hall, into the kitchen. Ruth has her back towards him at the sink. Absently, she reaches for a glass, not even looking up at the shelf, just reaching, glancing out the window.

Ruth runs the water without asking him if he wants any. So much for the welcome.

'Are you hungry?' he says to her back, to break the silence. 'I couldn't face plane food so I'm ravenous.'

There's nothing in the fridge, he's already checked, she

is not one to have food in. Ruth turns to face him and for a second holds his gaze, then switches, it's like he can hear the gear shift, she opens the fridge, shakes her head.

It's simpler if he says nothing, if he just dials.

'Hi, an order for delivery, please.' It sounds too loud, too bright in the room. Ruth has gone back to staring out the window, or at them, reflected in it. He sees the vague white shape of the rose, still blooming. It had been a warm summer in the end, after a disastrous start.

'Thanks.' Aidan hangs up. 'It'll be forty minutes.'

It seems an outrageously long time.

8.13 pm

I CAN'T BELIEVE YOU'RE VIOLATING MY TRUST LIKE THIS
PEN, WE HAVE A DEAL
ARE YOU OKAY?? TEXT ME BACK
PEN WHERE ARE YOU?

There are two violins, though one is larger so maybe it is a viola. A small guitar too. A cello. A double bass. Two pianos, somehow. Each instrument makes a different noise, but it is not like chaos in your brain, it is like making sense of the world because this is the sound of the world. And the notes are up and down, up and down, with an invisible line that seems to string the notes together. What does the world sound like? A mournful slow wail from the strings and the soft drum, a key striking on the piano, and together they are like the sound of connection. Down, down she goes, following them until a shaker lifts her up, and the man at the piano quivers his head back and forward.

Alice is sitting next to her and Pen reaches for her hand and Alice squeezes her fingers and they are one.

Alice is not sitting next to her and Pen clenches her fists on her thighs, braced for what this feeling is.

The musicians change instruments and begin a song the leader calls 'Protection', he says it changes every time they play it because at some point they get lost. Pen wonders how this happens, that they could get lost, because it must be written down or planned so if they still get lost maybe it means they want to.

Pen had texted Claire back.

OKAY. AT A CONCERT. IT WAS A SURPRISE FOR ALICE.

But the vibrations had kept coming. So even though the usher on the way in had said, 'Please turn off your phone,' Pen knew she had to talk to Claire. It was okay, she thought, because it was still early, and she was the only one sitting in her row.

'Hi, Mum.'

'Pen, I said you could go to the demonstration, but a concert?'

'Mmhmm,' which is what Pen says when she doesn't know what to say.

'Why didn't you tell me, I've been worried!'

'Mmhmm.'

'It's Monday-night pizza, it's your favourite.'

The notes of her mum's words were strained, alternating between high and low, sharp and blunt.

'This is really not okay, Pen. And what kind of an example is it for Soraya?'

Claire sighed and Pen thought that it wasn't fair to hurt someone else just because you were hurting, but that's what she has done to Claire by not coming home.

Now, the group are playing a song called 'Found Harmonium', and Pen thinks, oh, it is not just music for the lost. The harmonium looks like a box so it should be a piano, but it sounds like the wind through trees, noisy trees, like an organ, that's the right word. The music is like a wash of tiny moments.

Claire's voice got louder.

'I'm going to drive in to get you and Alice, no-arguments-young-lady.'

Pen had not heard that voice in ages.

'Alice isn't here.'

'What, Pen?'

'I'm on my own. And,' Pen looked up at the ceiling, 'other teenagers do this all the time, go to things on their own. It's safe, Mum.'

Claire exhaled loudly, for so long that it was amazing there was that much air inside her lungs, and then it was silent, them just breathing, and Pen imagined her mother, in the hall, car keys in her hand, leaning against the wall.

'Okay, Pen, okay,' Claire said. 'You haven't been drinking, right?'

'No.'

'And you'll get the bus home at nine, I don't care what's going on, you come home and if it's at all scary, or you're freaking out, just get a taxi and I'll pay him when he gets here. Okay?'

'Okay.'

'This doesn't mean everything is forgiven, Pen, there will still be consequences,' Claire said, but then her voice changed. 'But you may as well be hung for a sheep as a lamb.'

And that's when Pen knew it really was okay. Because she could still smile, and her mother could still laugh, at the ridiculous way language works. Pen is a teenage girl not a stealer of sheep, or lambs, she has never stolen anything.

The man onstage turns to the audience and his face is quite small and far away but she can still see it, and he says this song is called 'The Life of an Emperor', and Pen suddenly sees a blue sky with cirrus clouds and snow flats stretching to the horizon and she sees the notes stretching out between the sky and the snow, and music itself is almost visible if you think about it, reverberations, disturbances of the air, stretching between the bodies of the instruments and the body of the person bent over the vibrating wood and the head, the ear, her body, all their bodies.

Pen is sitting surrounded by people and no one needs her to talk or be or look a particular way. She risks looking at the people near her. Their faces are blank, unreadable. Which maybe means every single person is just being themselves. Pen wonders if they can see what she can see, if she sits really still and lets the vibrations happen, a building with spaces and columns rising in the empty space above their heads. And she wonders if they can see themselves and their lives.

The notes are coming into her body and the musicians don't really look at the audience, they look down at their instruments, at their music stands. Not out at the people. Pen imagines that some of them are like her. Quiet.

Once Alice had shown Pen a notebook filled with words, with lists of words. Confused, Pen had stayed still. 'They're lists of what I'm grateful for,' said Alice, 'my parents make me keep the lists when I get a blue.' She had paused, Pen had held on.

'They're to keep me grounded.'

'Do they work?'

'Not like they'd hope. They want me to be okay.'

'Parents always want you to be okay.' Pen had thought of her mother driving her every week to the woman-therapist's office. 'They don't know, that's all.'

Alice had said she was tired of pretending and Pen felt like she had been let in, to the space of not-pretending.

Everyone thinks that Alice is not quiet, that Alice is the opposite of Pen. But that is because they are in the pretending space and Pen is not. Alice told Pen that she just wanted to blend in, that was why she went with the gang, because it was a way of not being seen (no one is looking at you). Alice is not like the others, though she is pretty and popular, so you could make the mistake of thinking she is into showing off, but actually the real Alice is quiet. Which is why Pen likes her. Liked. Likes.

'Look at your hands, Pen.' It was meant to give you a feeling of control. Her hands on her thighs, pink with shiny nails against the denim. Alice had asked her if she did, like, manicures, 'You have really nice nails, Pen.' But Pen said, 'No, they just grow like that.' Alice's mum takes her to get their nails done, 'girls together', and Alice pulled a face when she said that and Pen kind of laughed, which was one of the first times they had ever really talked or shared something.

But there are no vibrations from her.

No text saying, wait for me. No text taking back the no, the look, the cold shoulder.

9.15 pm

Their movements are practised, yet somehow uncertain. Aidan watches as Ruth collects the plates, sets them in rows in the dishwasher. He folds the lids of the takeaway cartons, squashes them into the bin. Hears his own breathing, the ticking of the kitchen clock. They have barely spoken.

'Would you like tea?'

Aidan nods, thinking he could make an excuse, escape upstairs to unpack.

Ruth fills the kettle, sets it on its base, flicks the switch. Aidan stands, shuffles, leans against the kitchen island, watching the kettle. It's like a first date, this feeling. Or a last date. The kettle snaps off, but Ruth doesn't move.

'Do you want me to do it?' Aidan asks, allowing himself a note of exasperation.

Ruth turns to him, and he sees there are tears in her eyes, and they are both silent for a moment.

'What's wrong, Aidan?'

'Are you really telling me you don't know?'

They have begun.

'Do you still want tea?' Ruth asks.

'Okay.'

Ruth pours water into two mugs. Swirls. Squeezes. Milk in. She hands Aidan the cup. They are both careful, he notices, not to touch the other's hand, and his arm lurches slightly at the thought. A little tea spills. It's no good, Aidan can't say it. *He has to say it.*

'I think I'm getting a mouth ulcer,' Aidan says, and watches Ruth wince.

'Oh no,' she says, stretching out a hand, rubbing the backs of his fingers.

And it is easy for a moment for Aidan to believe that they are not afraid of each other, that Ruth can soothe them both by rubbing his hand, that this one action will fix them, and perhaps he won't have to say the real thing. She withdraws her hand, and he feels almost bereft.

Ruth can't keep her hand over his, not when it lies so inert on the counter like that, not when he shows no sign of knowing she's even touching him. It's always like this, oh god, it always feels like this, even when she reaches out it's cold cold cold.

Selfish, that's the word Aidan wants to say. Selfish. But how can he? It was her body, Ruth was right. Christ, she's smiling now. He knows it's a reflex, something she does when she's nervous. It used to drive her mother crazy, she'd told him, and for once he agrees with that woman, because it's hard to believe, looking at Ruth now, that she's taking it seriously. That she has any idea of how his heart is breaking.

Ruth is thinking, *I believe in you*, and she smiles but Aidan looks like he's about to turn away, and it will be lost, this moment, she will be lost. Her hand slaps down on his again, slap against the wooden counter, slap against his knuckles and they are both surprised at this action, which belongs to her hand.

'Selfish.' Aidan knows he's said it out loud because her face wrinkles. 'You were selfish. Are. You are. Selfish.'

'When?' Ruth's hand stays on his out of sheer stubbornness.

'When you decided that only your opinion mattered, that it was only your body, that it was. That it was . . . That it was over.'

'I couldn't do it any more, Aidan.'

'What about me?'

'You said, okay,' Ruth sighs. 'You said you were okay with it, Aidan, you said, let's take a break.'

'You were crying, shouting, you were – you remember – you were pounding your whole body with your fists, I thought you'd do yourself an injury, I was afraid. So I said yes. But this,' and Aidan pulls his hand away from hers to point at her, 'this isn't a break! So what choice am I left with now, to be, to be the dickhead who forces you to try, who forces you to be pregnant—'

'Don't you mean to be not pregnant?' Ruth stares at him, face belligerent. 'Not pregnant again? Because we've been there, we have tried, and it was all for nothing.' Her hands are held out wide, taking it all in.

'It was not, not for nothing,' something clenches inside Aidan. 'It was for us, for our child, that we tried.'

'Don't you think I know that?'

'I'm not sure what you know, Ruth. Seriously.' But Ruth does not move an inch and Aidan decides to let it out. 'On the trip,' he waves his hand back to suggest the recent past, 'on the trip one of the guys asked – you think men don't get asked, but they do – the guy asked if I had kids. And every time that happens, I just freeze inside. What can I say to him, this guy I don't even know that well? That we wanted to, that we tried, but it didn't happen for us? I couldn't, I couldn't even bring myself to say no.'

'What did you say?'

'I just shook my head,' and Aidan repeats the gesture now at Ruth.

'I'm sure he got it.'

'I'm sure he fucking didn't. Do you know what he said? He said, "Aren't you the smart one, kids are a nightmare, mate, you're so lucky being able to do what you want." And he slapped me on the back. I could have punched him.'

'Oh, Aidan, I'm so sorry.'

'Are you, though?' Aidan lets it hang for a moment. 'We could have tried Spain or Prague, they have better results, other people manage it.'

'And some other people are destroyed by it!'

'And what are we? What are we, Ruth? Happy? Well, you are, you're *fine*, look at you, you're moving forward, it's just me left behind.'

He is almost panting with hostility. They stand on either side of the room, like boxers in their corners.

'I went to the hospital alone today, Aidan.'

Aidan looks blank, then knowledge dawning. 'That was today.'

'That was today. I'm fine, in case you're wondering.'

'I'm sorry, I forgot. Sorry. I mean, that's good.' Aidan rubs the back of his head, trying to dislodge something. Why does it always feel like a competition between them? As if she has heard this thought, Ruth shifts and sighs, sliding her cup of tea from side to side on its coaster.

'You really think I'm selfish? Selfish with my bruised body, selfish with the daily injections, with the hormone swings, selfish? Easy for you, standing there, holding my hand, but you didn't have to go through any of it – oh, jizz in a cup, how humiliating for you, but probes and needles and all, into me, inside me – it was so debasing, I felt, and you never even asked, you just kept saying it would be worth it in the end, but you didn't see me, you didn't see what it cost me, because it was what you wanted. I'm not the selfish one.'

'That's not fair, I was there, and you never wanted to talk, you just went to bed, or you snapped at me, and I – I left you alone, because it was what you wanted.' He can't look at her, he has to look at his feet, he is more ashamed than he thought possible, because surely he is in the right, surely his feelings count too? 'Remember?' he wants to ask her, but he can't, remember how it felt to have those months of being parents? He'd thought they were in it together. But then a year ago, Ruth had shouted at him outside the doctor's office, had shouted that she wouldn't do it any more, and he knew that he was alone in this.

'Sometimes, honestly, Ruth, it's like sometimes I think you don't regret it.'

'Regret it?'

'How it turned out, that you're relieved it didn't work. You can give everything to your practice this way.'

Ruth wants to slap him, to tell him that he must-be-fucking-joking. She exhales. 'Do you know the term for me, for women like me? They call people like me, wombs like mine, a hostile environment.'

'But it worked once. We were just unlucky!'

'There were so many days it was a struggle to get out of bed,' Ruth says, 'it was like an assault every time someone asked me how I was, and I had to say, "Fine." It was more than I could bear.'

'And my body?' Aidan demands. 'You never ask about mine. About the way I ached from not sleeping. About carrying this emotion every day. And yes, I did tests too, not as bad as yours, but still, every moment, wondering, "Is it me?"' Aidan pauses, but Ruth just looks back at him. 'And at the clinic, at the hospital, when you turned down the counselling, did you know that I asked for it?'

'When?'

'Later, I went back later. I made an appointment and the therapist came out, expecting both of us, I guess. She looked at me like I'd said something obscene when she realised it was just me. Apparently, partners are only allowed with the mother.'

'Aidan. I didn't know. I really didn't – I'm sorry.'

'You abandoned me,' Aidan's voice is louder than he'd meant, and he sees the shock on Ruth's face.

'I'm sorry,' Ruth begins to say, but no, she can't do it, she can't get stuck in this loop *sorry sorry sorry*, it feels like she is erasing herself. She takes a moment. Where else can they go? She looks at him but he has gone back to staring at the floor.

'Aidan, what if we did it again?'

Aidan looks up at her, unable to believe what he's hearing.

'What if we did it again?'

The sounds begin to knit together into some kind of meaning as Aidan realises she is asking him a question. *Hope. Fear.*

'What if I said yes,' Ruth says, 'let's do it again. What if we try and we try and we give it everything, one more time? And what if we do it, but still, it does not work.' Ruth pauses. 'Aidan? Would you be able to stop then?'

It is not a fair question. Aidan clears his throat. It is not fair because if they did it again, if it did not work, he could not go on. The wave is not fear or hope now, it's despair. He has to hold on to the worktop edge. What is she saying now?

'What if we really are time travellers? I know, it's mad. But what if we are in the future, a different future, and I am saying to you, yes, we did it again, and we put all our hope in that last attempt, and yet still, Aidan, still it didn't work.' Ruth is shaking with the effort. 'What if we did five or six or seven cycles and still it didn't work?'

Aidan is sinking, not even fighting the waves.

'I can imagine it, that other future, how we would lose more of ourselves each time and still we would not have what we wanted. And you would still be standing there, looking at me, asking for more. How many times would have been enough for you?' Ruth pauses, and feels the vibrations in the air of the words that are her husband's worst nightmare. 'You would never have given up, Aidan.'

He is not breathing, he is underwater.

'We tried, we gave it everything, Aidan.'

His lungs hurt.

'We kept trying, we just got the wrong answer every time.'

He will never survive this.

'We got the answer we didn't want.'

His whole body, now, underwater.

'I had to make the call.'

She has come around to where he is, she is standing beside him, looking at him, and Aidan can't speak or cry or breathe.

'And I am so sad about it, I carry that grief too, but you have to forgive me, Aidan. To forgive both of us.'

It is like he is part of the water.

'Aidan, listen to me. I forgive you.'

Perhaps the tide recedes slightly.

'It's not your fault, Aidan. None of this is your – anyone's – fault.'

The top of his head is free now.

'Aidan, you need to forgive me, to forgive yourself.'

He takes a breath.

'We can get through this,' Ruth says, her hands opening up in an appeal. 'If we try at that – at *this* – instead.'

He clears his throat, aware of the dry air. He is in their kitchen, hand on the wooden worktop that he and Ruth had chosen for their home, the home that he thought he'd share with his children.

'You have to forgive us both, Aidan.'

'Time travellers,' he says.

'Maybe,' Ruth's voice is small. She must know she has gone too far.

Aidan stands still, feeling the remnants of the lie that the wave has swept away, the lie that he has told himself every day, the lie that he has used as a shield for so long. The hope that was also a lie, that it would have worked *next time*. He looks at Ruth and sees the smudge of mascara under her eyes, the strands of hair escaping from a bun, the mark of glasses on her nose.

'We are time travellers, Ruth,' Aidan says, and he can hear the water rushing again. 'But we don't go forward, we go back.' He pauses, feeling the wave inside him. He looks at Ruth and he sees her defenceless face, sees how hard she is trying, and it is true, she has given it everything. But it hurts too much.

'In this time machine, we go back to the past. Can you imagine that, Ruth? We go back a year and a half, to the last time you said you needed a break. Remember?'

Ruth gives a small nod.

'And if we go back, in this magical vision of yours, tell me, Ruth, can you take back what you said about our last embryo?'

Ruth looks at him.

'In your fantasy about time, can you make it so that you never said what you said about our last embryo?'

'What, Aidan?' Ruth shakes her shoulders as if to dislodge something. 'What are you talking about?'

'I said that we couldn't leave it, couldn't stop, when we still had an embryo left.'

'We didn't "leave it". We used it. It didn't implant.'

'But before that, when I was begging you, when I was saying that it was our cells, our flesh and blood in that freezer. You don't remember what you said?'

Ruth only shakes her head.

'You said, "If it's so bad to imagine your 'flesh and blood' in a freezer, then we can ask the clinic to dispose of it." '

He sees the weight of it land on her, sees her remember.

'I was scared, Aidan.'

'Or maybe,' and Aidan speaks the thing he has never allowed himself to think before, 'maybe you never really wanted a baby.'

Ruth stands very still, holding herself in case the smallest movement shatters her. It is always the person who knows you best, who sees you best, who loves you best, who turns around and hurts you the most.

All day the voices in her head, alternating.

Run! Stay!

9.25 pm

LEESON STREET (PEMBROKE STREET)
LEESON STREET BRIDGE

46A, top deck, front seat.

SUSSEX ROAD
MOREHAMPTON ROAD (MARLBOROUGH ROAD)
BUS GARAGE
DONNYBROOK CHURCH

The bus makes its usual noise, the engine loud when the road goes up a hill, the window-rattle, the kids on the back seats laughing, the indicator blinking because they're stopping, the doors swish-bang, the voice saying the fare, you can't hear where, the beep of their travel card, the noise on the stairs as they come up, holding on when the bus pulls out, accelerates, the squeak and squish of them sitting down, and then it's just the engine again. Whine, whirr, whoosh.

WELLINGTON PLACE. *Wellie Boot Place more like*, saying that is one of the ways Pen can make Soraya laugh, that's a good feeling. And thinking this makes Pen care less that she'd had to leave the concert early, that she'd had to push past people whose faces didn't look very pleased, that she'd had to walk through the lobby hearing the music still going on behind her. But perhaps Pen had got what she needed anyway because she feels like her body is still vibrating which means she is carrying the music in her.

STILLORGAN ROAD. NUTLEY LANE. Flyover to the university where her mum works, Green Apple garage, all those apartment blocks, still with the hoarding telling you about elegant-living-in-south-Dublin, 'What do they think is so "elegant"?' her mum says every time. 'They're just apartments overlooking a dual carriageway.' Cars on the road, going where? All the houses, every house, every car is lives, all their lives, every person believing in the specialness of their own life. WOODBINE ROAD. SEAFIELD ROAD. WOODLANDS AVENUE. Feel them, name them, know them. Keep them in your body with the music.

STILLORGAN BYPASS, whose syllables clang. The Stillorgan Bowl. Where Pen had had a meltdown and someone had filmed it and Claire had complained and the manager had said, 'Look, lady, no one makes you bring your weird kid here.' More apartments. 'Uninspiring,' her dad says in her head, and it makes Pen feel funny-strange to think of her parents who-are-not-together-any-more saying things that sound the same. And it feels even funnier, even stranger, to realise that they are both wrong. Because the lives inside, they are elegant, they are inspiring. MERVILLE ROAD, GALLOPING GREEN.

Foxrock Church where the little girl's funeral was. All the people had had empty faces and afterwards Claire had said, 'That's what shock looks like, Pen,' and her voice had been really tired. They'd seen Pen's woman-therapist at the church so she must have known the family too. You weren't meant to talk to your therapist outside of sessions, it was a privacy thing, which was good because the church was really crowded and Pen was happier outside in the car park, but she thinks about this every time the bus turns at Foxrock Church, of all the people who came that day to be sad together. She knows Claire thinks it too, because sometimes, when they drive past, she will say the girl's name under her breath, and blink a lot, and Pen thinks she is trying to keep her alive somehow, because people vibrate too. At their next session, Pen had said she was sorry-for-your-loss, and the woman-therapist had thanked her and then said it was good to cry, good to let yourself mourn. She wasn't talking about herself, Pen knew. Sometimes the woman-therapist uses outside examples and Pen knows that really it's about her. Happy can be hard to show, but being sad is even harder, it's like a weight on your chest. It's what Alice calls 'a big blue'. Pen looked that one up and told Alice, who said she liked it better in Latin. *Magnum caeruleum.* Maybe Pen needs to stop saying 'the woman' bit before 'therapist', lots of people, it turns out, see therapists.

'Do you ever stand in the shower and let the hot water just fall on you?' she'd asked Alice once. Alice had nodded and said, 'I turn the nozzle thing on the shower and it's good for putting on your neck and if you close your eyes it's like you can't tell where the water starts and your body ends,' and Pen had nodded back. She had been so close to Alice then that she had nearly told her about how sometimes when she was standing under the water like that, she touched the scars of the cuts on her thighs. How it made her heart go faster, but also made her feel empty. That was the point of cutting, it made all the bad stuff empty out of you, but then it made the good stuff go too. That was what the therapist told her.

The cutting had started after Lauren's house and Pen

hadn't even done it much, but Soraya saw her one day, saw the dried blood on her thighs, when she came into their bedroom and Pen wasn't dressed. 'Mum,' Soraya had yelled, and Pen had been really angry with her, and screamed and cried, but now she can see that her baby sister did the right thing.

Claire had talked to them both one night soon after that. Had told them that Sandy was going to be staying with John-at-work till he got his own place, and that they would get their own place too. Soraya had cried then, but Pen had just nodded and said okay. When Soraya had gone to bed, Claire had asked Pen to stay and talk a little longer. Then she'd said, 'Pen, let's make a deal.' She had told Pen that she was a wise soul, and that with her dad not there any more, though she was only fifteen, it was like she was the other adult. So Claire needed her to take some responsibility, not just household chores, she meant for the family, for being in the family. Claire had spoken slowly and softly, looking at the window, not Pen. All the time Claire was talking, Pen had wanted to ask what had gone wrong, why was her dad moving out, was it her? But she didn't, because she knew that Claire would say, no, love, it wasn't you, sometimes two adults and on and on. Even though the answer probably was her. So she said okay to the deal, which was that they would all do their best by each other, and they would not keep secrets from each other, because their family came first. And Claire had been right, it did get better. Maybe Pen was calmer without her dad around, without the fighting. Maybe the therapy helped, the sense that she was not wrong, that she was just herself. Maybe Claire was right about another thing too, that you could only really be yourself when you let people in, when you let people see you.

DEAN'S GRANGE CROSS, and Pen in her high seat looks out over the scene and they used to live near here, before the new house, but Pen prefers living closer to the sea, and when she said it to Claire recently, that now they could walk by the sea every day so it didn't matter that they didn't have a garden any more, Claire's face had smoothed out and Pen thought that had been a good thing to say.

BAKER'S CORNER, KILL AVENUE FIRE STATION, CAR-RIGLEA COURT and the art college that Soraya would always point to when they go past because she wants to make things, and Claire would say, 'Where do I get these wonderful daughters from?' Pen used to think that wasn't true, that Claire didn't really think that about her. She had said something about it to her therapist once. 'Do you really believe that?' the therapist had asked. Pen had shaken her head. 'Can you say it?' she asked. 'No,' Pen said and then, when the therapist kept looking at her with her gentle face, Pen said, 'My mum thinks I'm wonderful.'

Ring the bell. Go down the steps. Stand near the driver. The bus will go on without her, down York Road, Crofton Road, to the station where Pen was this morning when everything seemed possible.

TIVOLI ROAD. Where did the name Tivoli come from? 'Oh, good question, Pen,' Claire had said, and talked about Copenhagen and Paris and Rome, and Pen loves this about her mother, all the things she knows, all the ways of telling them the world is made for them.

Pen turns into her street, sees the locksmith's and the mechanic's. Sandy always says they were lucky to buy when they did, but he doesn't say it in a nice way, and when Soraya reported it back, Pen said maybe it meant he was jealous, and then Claire said, 'Hard cheese.' Pen thinks of how Claire grates up cheese that's been around too long and puts it on bread under the grill and it softens up again and how maybe her dad is like that, he needs something to make him softer, though it is not Pen, or Soraya, or Claire.

The light is shining over their front door and Pen's key fits into the lock and her mum is in the hall.

'You're home.'

Pen looks at her mother, at the narrow stairs, at the pile of shoes by the skirting. And it is too much.

Pen walks towards Claire and lowers her face and butts the top of her head against her mother's collarbone and she is really home. They stand touching like this, they are breathing together again, being again, and being in silence, which Pen is good at, and her mother bad at. Pen lifts her head and sees Soraya a few stairs from the top, leaning on the old handrail that wobbles, not saying anything, standing in her pink pyjamas and sighing slightly before walking back to her room.

'Mum,' Pen whispers into the shoulder, and she does not know what to say but just 'Mum' might be enough.

Alice stands at the corner, waiting to cross. Perhaps she should go down further, where there are lights, but also perhaps there will be a break in the traffic soon. She feels a little drunk.

'Was Pen feeling okay?' Jo had asked, and Alice had nodded. After that, it felt both easy and hard to stay in the pub and listen to the conversation go on, though Alice hadn't really talked much. When they went round the corner to Talbot Street to get chips, it still seemed normal to keep with the group. 'Did you know,' Jo kept saying, 'did you know that most of the potatoes in chippers aren't actually grown in Ireland?' A few people made jokes about the Famine, and Alice laughed along, except she was really thinking about Pen. Why couldn't she have just gone with her?

'We're heading back to the tents,' Jo said after they'd wolfed their chips and spice burgers. 'We probably shouldn't have stayed away so long.'

Alice nodded, noticing that the others were standing slightly apart.

'So, do you want to come back with us?'

Alice looked away. 'I should probably head home.'

'Early night?'

'Yeah, I guess.' Alice realised she should say something

else, Jo looked like she was waiting for something. 'It was really cool, though, thanks.'

'Maybe we could, like, swap numbers,' Jo said. 'So we can stay in touch about protests and stuff.'

Alice nodded, but said, 'I've no battery, sorry.' Even though she knew her phone was fine.

'Just tell me yours, then,' Jo said, screen lighting up, ready.

'086,' Alice started, though her number was 087.

A bus pulls in, and Alice realises she's standing at a stop, she'll never get across here. She walks a little further down.

'Hey! Hey, you! Do you know which way to Marino?'

There is a car stopped by the kerb, and the driver is leaning across, shouting at Alice. Grey car. Maybe silver, hard to tell in the yellow-lighted street. The driver smiles. So Alice walks over.

'Sorry?'

'Do you know which way,' the man gestures at the road, 'to get to Marino?'

'Oh, yeah, it's—'

What is wrong with this picture?

Man, smiling. Dials lit up on the dashboard. Coat crumpled on the passenger seat. His hand on the seat as he leans forward. Alice bends down so she can see him, it.

It.

His other hand.

'Oh,' Alice feels frozen.

His other hand is moving. Something at the front of his jeans. Hand. Pulling.

'Oh,' Alice moves back, a jerking movement. A wave of nausea. Away from the car, the leering man.

Standing, looking around now, no people really near, maybe Alice should shout. But her voice won't come.

The car shifts, ever so slowly, closer to the kerb. The window draws up to Alice again.

Pounding. This is the word. It is like noticing something strange about yourself, like being two people. One who can see everything happening and the other, this body, which will not move to save itself. Alice's eyes slide back to the window. And there is another thing to notice. He has not stopped smiling, has not stopped his hand moving, he is leering more widely. Alice knows, and does not know how she knows, but she knows that her reaction is part of what he wants.

Alice steps back, swaying a bit, then halts again. She might curl into a tiny ball. She might cry. She wishes, oh, she wishes, Pen were here. Strong, kind Pen.

And then the man says, 'Hey, get in.'

What should she do?

'Are you alright, love?'

A woman is standing beside Alice, and she's only barely finished asking it, but the car is already zooming off.

'Was he some kind of perv?'

'Yeah. I mean, yeah, he was —' and Alice gestures to the front of her trousers.

'What a prick!'

'Yeah,' Alice says, a little more herself now. 'Thanks for being—'

'You want to watch out for stuff like that, young girl like you.'

'I'm on my way to the Dart,' Alice says, feeling stupid, and the woman nods.

'Go on, then, you're grand now.'

'Thanks. Bye.'

The station is quiet but it's after ten so maybe that's normal. Alice goes through the ticket gates and along the walkway to where it branches. Staircase to her right, passageway under the tracks ahead. She looks up at the displays.

3 MINS to Howth.

1 MIN to Bray.

She could go either way. Home? Or to Pen?

The display for the train to Bray flickers, then goes blank.

10.26 pm

'Do you want to tell me what happened?'

They are sitting on the sofa and the notes of Claire's voice are soft.

Pen can't speak.

'Did you and Alice have a falling-out?'

Pen can't speak.

'You can nod, Pen.'

Pen half-nods.

'Was it during the rally? Alice sounded very concerned for you on the phone. God, I wish you'd come home then, or I'd collected you.'

None of these are questions, so Pen does not respond.

'Did Alice want to go home?'

Shakes head.

'At what point did Alice go home?'

Pen shrugs.

'Pen, I need something more from you. You and Alice were meant to go to a concert, it was a secret, but she didn't want to go?'

Claire's voice is harder now, the notes sound brittle. Pen nods.

'So Alice changed her mind, went home and you stayed in town by yourself?'

Pen shakes her head.

'Which bit, Pen?'

'In the pub.'

'You went to the pub?'

The notes of Claire's voice go up. Pen nods.

'By yourself?'

Pen shakes.

'Who with? What pub? I know you're sixteen, Pen, but pubs?' Pen starts to pull away from Claire. 'Okay, okay,' Claire holds up her hands.

Perhaps if Pen could open her brain somehow and let her mother see inside, but that was actually impossible. Perhaps if other people could open their brains so Pen could see, but that was just as impossible. Claire is waiting while Pen stares at the floor.

'So you were in the pub, and Alice decided to go home instead of to the concert. But you wanted to hear the band or whatever, so you went alone. Wow, Pen.'

'Alice didn't go home.'

'What do you mean?'

'She stayed in the pub.'

'Wait, what?'

The notes are even higher now. Pen does not move.

'You left Alice in a pub alone, alone by herself?'

The notes fall, like this is serious. Nod. Shake.

'Not by herself.'

'Who with?'

'Jo.' Pause. 'Other people.'

'Jo?'

'Your student.'

'My student, I have hundreds of—oh, okay, second-year-climate-Jo.' Claire breathes. 'Pen, was Alice drinking?'

Notes up and down, up and down. Nods.

'Have you heard from her since?'

Miserable. Shake.

'Can you phone her now?'

More miserable. Shake.

Pen's mum is standing, picking up her phone from the coffee table, scrolling.

'Give me Alice's number.'

Notes down, definitely down. Pen leans forward. 'No, Mum.'

'Don't "No, Mum" me. You won't tell me what happened,' and the notes are all the same now. 'I mean, Jo is a good student but what's she doing hanging around with kids?'

Pen has no idea how to answer this question.

'Come on, Pen, give me her number. Just to make sure she's alright.'

Pen doesn't move for a moment. Then she holds up the screen towards her mum. Claire looks up and down, putting in the numbers. Presses the green phone icon. Shakes her head. Hangs up.

'It didn't go through.'

Claire has her puzzled face on. Pen looks at her screen, presses the green phone, listens. The-customer-has-their-phone-powered-off.

Alice never runs out of battery, never turns her phone off.

Alice walking away, Alice in the pub, Alice I'll have a pint, Alice drunk, Alice alone or with someone not nice, Alice in danger. Pen's breath has stopped, she presses the green phone again. Pen's mother sitting next to Pen, stroking her back.

'Breathe in and out, in-breath, out-breath. Okay, Pen.'

And Pen is the worst person ever because it never occurred

to her, not once did she think that Alice did not leave her, that Pen was the one who left.

'In-breath, out-breath.'

Stroke, stroke. Stim, stim, but not gentle, palm against leg, more like stam-stam-stam.

'I'm sure she's fine.'

Stroke, stroke, stam-stam-stam-stam-stam.

She left Alice.

10.31 pm

'You remember,' Ruth begins, 'you remember that I had a temperature and I had to go in to have a final scan? And that after the scan they said that all the products of conception weren't clear?' Aidan looks at her, he looks like he's underwater, and if things were otherwise, she would ask him if he is alright, if he's drowning, but she will not stretch out her hand again.

'I'm sorry, I don't know, which bit,' Aidan says.

'After the miscarriage, after they'd told us that the womb wasn't clear.' Ruth watches him access the memory. She sees them, as if from across a great distance, sitting in the dim room, blinds closed for privacy, making it a cave. How could he forget the warnings of sepsis, the look of worry, the speed with which the midwife got a doctor?

'They were worried about, well, about lots of things, and they said I should have a D&C. Do you remember now?'

Aidan half-shakes, half-nods his head.

'So I went into hospital the next day. When I came round afterwards you were sitting by the bed, and the nurse told you I could go home if I could walk to the loo by myself. You had to help me, but I managed it, and we got a taxi home, and I just went to bed. Do you remember?'

There is only grief stretched across Aidan's face and she knows it is because she's making him remember the worst week of his life.

'I think, I felt,' Ruth pauses because she might break apart, she might break any second now, into a million tiny unrecoverable pieces, 'I felt like it was the last bad thing that I could take. Like with all the scans and now surgery, I had been abused somehow. Or spoiled, maybe that's it.'

Aidan shakes his head, in sorrow or disagreement, it is hard to tell.

'I felt like some vital part of me was being removed, that I was losing myself,' Ruth tries again. 'I know, I mean, I know what a counsellor would say, that I was losing a baby, that I was losing my sense of control, that my feelings were a reaction to those things happening to me against my will,' Ruth inhales. 'But I didn't want to be told that, to have explanations. I just knew that I couldn't keep doing this to myself.'

'I'm sorry, Ruth,' Aidan's voice is quiet. 'But isn't that why counselling would be good, isn't that exactly why?'

'I know, I know, you're right,' Ruth agrees, though the feeling inside her doesn't change. Is she asking for the moon, for her husband to be on her side?

'But I felt like my body knew it too. Aidan, listen. I felt like I shouldn't have had the D&C. I know it's irrational. But I felt something change in me – like they'd scraped out too much of me. And I never said anything to you, to the doctors, but I thought it over and over. I am *broken*. My body and my mind were just reflecting the same thing. And I knew it would never happen because I had nothing left for it. Do you see, Aidan? Do you understand?'

They stand in silence. The water is gone, the air is gone, it is just them, alone together, damaged and heartsore.

'Ruth, that makes no sense. They do that procedure on thousands of women, if it made a difference they would know, the doctors would know, they would have said something on the last cycle,' Aidan pauses to collect himself. 'And this feeling, it's natural. Christ, it's not like I didn't feel it too. But stopping wasn't going to cure that.'

Silence again. Aidan looks at his hands, at the wall, at anything it seems, but Ruth.

She has told him everything now. So how is he still not touching her? How is it still not enough?

10.32 pm

The shrill sound is not coming out of Pen.

'Keep breathing, Pen,' Claire says over her shoulder as she goes into the hall. The front door clicks. 'Oh, Alice!'

And Pen is standing but her feet won't move. Pen gets to the hall anyway, without her feet, maybe they are left behind in the living room. And there is Alice, her mother has her hands on Alice's shoulders, pulling her into the house. (*Ecce! In pictura est puella!*)

'Don't worry, no alarm.' Though the notes of Claire's voice say to everyone that they were worried.

Pen looks at Alice's face. Alice looks something Pen can't name except it looks like Soraya when she has broken something belonging to Pen.

'Your phone was off,' Pen says, and hears the harsh notes of her own voice.

And Alice replies, but not to Pen, she is speaking to Pen's mother. Something about coverage, and Pen can't listen or process because for ten seconds, for a minute, for more, Alice was hurt or lost or dead. And now Alice is alive.

'I'll make some tea,' Claire says, nodding at Pen, and then closing the door to the kitchen, which is never closed normally, but is being closed by Pen's mother now.

Alice smells of beer and outside.

Alice doesn't say anything and neither does Pen.

A moment. No notes, except breathing. Then Alice smiles a very small smile.

Alice has her phone and her earphones in her hands. She holds out one of the buds towards Pen and there is nothing extraordinary about it except Alice is standing in front of her with a new look on her face. Alice takes a step towards Pen, and another, and she's so close now Pen could lean forward and brush her lips across Alice's fringe.

Alice reaches her hand up and she is gentle as she fits the bud into Pen's left ear. She puts the other in her own ear, so they are sharing. Alice looks at Pen's face, so close, so close, and then down at her phone screen, she touches PLAY.

First, there is a pulsing keyboard, a steady beat. Almost the wind again in these notes. A high voice that can make the word 'sweet' last a whole bar, then 'gentle' and 'sensitive' and it sounds like the most beautiful noise ever as Kate Bush sings the word 'obsessive' like it is a heroic quality.

Alice is watching Pen's face. Trying to read her.

Guitar.

Chorus. 'Three,' the notes rise joyfully, 'point one four.'

The smile grows on Alice's face as she sways towards Pen, as they share Pen's favourite song. Pen's mother looks from the doorway, closes the door again.

10.50 pm

'Do you love me?'

'Ruth, what? Of course.'

'Are you sure?'

'What is this? Yes.'

' "Yes." ' Ruth raises her hands and lets them fall. 'What does that mean to you, Aidan? What does that even mean, if this is how you react?'

'My reaction? What about yours? Honestly, you act like it was just another decision, "No more trying." But it is our life, it is our whole life together.'

'You're so angry with me.' Ruth's voice comes out like a whisper.

'I'm not even – I'm not angry, Ruth. I'm disappointed.'

'I'm sorry, Aidan.'

' "Sorry." Seriously? Like we're *strangers*. Like you're not affected by any of this?'

'Didn't you hear what I just said, Aidan, don't you know that I blame myself?'

'It's not about blame. It was a procedure, you had to have it! You just said it, it's not anyone's fault.'

'You're missing the point.'

'Ruth, I was never trying to blame you.'

'But that's how it feels, Aidan. Come on, look at everything you say to me! It's like I'm only a baby incubator to you.' Ruth can't believe she's actually saying it. 'A broken incubator.'

Aidan only shakes his head at her, though at least he is finally looking at her.

'You're not broken, Ruth. Though maybe you want to be, maybe it makes it easier to justify to yourself. I don't know. I'm sorry, I don't even mean that.' Aidan shakes his head again.

Ruth can't take it any more and she has no plan, no truth, no answer, no idea of what to do. She leans forward and lays her forehead on the island between them, as if in supplication. The wood is hard, blotting out the world.

'I can't talk to you if you do that,' Aidan says.

'What do you want me to say?' Ruth's voice is muffled by the wood. 'Do you want me to say I'm happy?'

Her scalp shows through her hair, which has fallen to one side, spooling on the wood, the skin grey and pink. Aidan wants, strangely, to stroke it. He looks at the window, at their reflection, Ruth's head on the counter, him towering over her, both of them grotesque. How has he brought them to this?

'Ruth.'

'I can't really breathe like that,' Ruth says, rising up. Her face is red, the tip of her nose white, she wipes her eyes. 'Do you remember the Alhambra last year?'

Why must she always do this? Which was it, the miscarriage she felt guilty for, or that miserable trip to Spain? Which was the important thing?

'Do you remember,' she asks, 'there was some confusion with the coach at Malaga?'

'You'd organised tickets,' he says, despite himself.

'You were calm, that's what I remember,' Ruth says. She remembers frantically tapping at her phone, retrieving their booking, zooming in to see the details on the tiny screen. 'And you said we were in the right place and if we just waited, it would be okay.'

Aidan nods again.

'It was after we'd stopped,' Ruth says. Because it was after the fourth cycle.

'I thought we would keep going, later, I thought we would,' Aidan says.

'Do you remember the Nasrid Palace?' Ruth asks, because the voice in her head says, *stay*. Aidan looks blankly at her, but she will not give up. 'How hot it was and how I kept threatening to climb into one of the fountains?' Aidan grants her another nod. 'It could be like that again,' Ruth says.

'Like what, Ruth?' Aidan says.

'Good. Happy.'

Aidan looks at Ruth and there is the blank expression again.

'I don't mean,' Ruth says, 'just on holiday, I mean it was good because you were there.' Ruth pauses, because Aidan is giving her nothing, and she does not know how to say this next part. 'And still, I knew,' Ruth says, and her voice wavers with a long-held pain, 'I knew there was something missing. I kept thinking how much better it would have been to show it all to a child, all the carved screens and secret rooms, to dangle a baby's feet into the cool water. I kept getting these flashes, images of us, with our child. I wanted to be there as a family.'

This feeling. Aidan knows it. He had wanted the same, exactly the same.

'You never told me.' His voice sounds too sharp.

'I didn't know how to. And I couldn't bear to bring it up again, for either of us.' Ruth's face looks at him. She is leaning against the wooden counter, one hand resting on its surface.

'I thought you didn't care,' Aidan says, looking directly at her now. And suddenly he remembers. Not Granada, but the hospital room. Of how he had felt, too, that he could not go on.

Ruth gives a slight shake of her head.

'I thought that you'd moved on,' Aidan says, voicing the old accusations, but without conviction. 'You were working all the time.'

'I miss the children we did not have,' Ruth says, and there are tears in her eyes once more. 'I will never know our child, never hug them, or have a conversation with them, or look at them out in the world. I will never get to love them. I don't think I will ever be over that, Aidan, I don't think I will ever stop grieving that.'

It is almost too much, when you hear the thing you have waited so long, *too long*, to be spoken aloud. When you hear it and realise that you are not alone in your loss. How could he have persuaded himself she felt nothing? Aidan looks at his wife and feels, at last, a rush of love like a pang of grief. They could not go on, so she had said stop.

'I miss them too,' Aidan says. 'We both miss them.'

Pen's mother says Alice can stay the night, but they have to go to bed now because it's a school night and she is not going to be late tomorrow just because they've decided to go gallivanting. Even though the words are strict words, Pen thinks it's like Claire is laughing, like Claire and Pen are thinking the same thing: this is happy. Pen says she will sleep on the floor, Alice can have her bed, and Claire smiles again, but says they will not, repeat will not, be messing around talking or whatever. Claire nods her head then, saying Alice will be on the sofa bed down here and she'll make it up in a minute. Then Claire reminds Alice she has to call her parents to check it's okay, because she is not an enabler who will break other parents' rules. Pen hears Claire's sensible parent voice when she says this, and she smiles on the inside.

Alice and Pen have had tea and two rounds of cheese on toast with Marmite (Pen only, Alice doesn't like Marmite). Alice and Pen have talked, but also not talked. Which is okay, Pen doesn't need Alice to say anything. Because Pen is still not sure what's happening, but this kind of not-knowing somehow feels good. The opposite of the wardrobe day.

'There was a guy, in a car,' Alice says now, looking at the floor, and Pen feels her heart clench. 'He had his, his *dick* out, like, it was,' Alice shudders, 'it was gross, Pen.'

Pen doesn't know what to say, so she slowly raises her left

hand and puts it gently on the back of Alice's neck. Her hand rests on Alice's hair and it feels right. Alice is motionless, a beat of time passes, and Pen puts her hand back on her own leg. They breathe again.

'I couldn't think what to do,' Alice says in a small voice, 'so I came here.' She looks round at Pen, quickly, then away.

'Where was it?' Pen asks.

'Just by Connolly, you know, near the pub.'

Pen knows, and nods. 'If you got on at Connolly, that's eleven stops from here.' Which is totally the wrong thing to say.

'Yeah,' Alice says, and she seems to relax.

'Right, you two,' Claire shouts from the hallway. 'None of us is getting any younger, time for bed.'

Pen is lending Alice pyjamas and giving her a spare tooth-brush Claire bought on buy-one-get-one-half-price. Pen and Alice are brushing their teeth, quiet-but-the-okay-kind-of-quiet. Pen and Alice are leaning forward at the same time and almost hitting their heads. Pen and Alice are moving at the same time, their hips bumping together, their hands acciden-tally touching. It is amazing.

Alice gets changed in the bathroom and Pen gets changed in her room. Pen's wondering if she should wait on the land-ing, when Alice knocks on her door.

'Come in.'

Pen's heart thuds really hard as Alice pushes open the door, and for the moment that they stand looking at each other she thinks Alice must be able to hear it, but that's not possible, it only vibrates inside Pen. Alice is looking at Pen and it is the longest Pen has held eye contact ever. Alice looks down first, as if she is trying to see her feet better. Her toes are small and pale pink and the nails are short and perfect.

'I feel really stupid. I should have gone to the concert, it was so nice of you to give me a surprise.'

'It was okay.'

'I'm glad you had a good time, that the band were, like, good. Maybe next time, we can go.'

Pen nods.

'I guess I was just confused by the date part, I mean.'

'We can be friends if that's what you want.'

Say no. Say that is not what you want. Say you want me.

'I like you so much, Pen, you can't know how much, how important.'

'You like Jo instead.' Pen had not meant to say it. Alice's face looks up and her eyes are wider than normal.

'Jo? No, I mean, she's nice. I just. They're different, you know, and they don't know me. So I can. I could be different around them.'

'You can be different around me.'

'I know. But not really,' Alice says. 'I don't know what I mean, really.'

Pen shifts her weight from one foot to the other. And there is a silence now, a different kind of silence than before. Alice is looking around and, for once, Pen doesn't feel like she's the one who can't find the words. Her therapist always reminds Pen that it's not just her, everyone struggles, that some words are harder to say than others.

'Do you want to write it down?' Pen asks.

And Alice looks up at her and it looks like hope on her face. Hope and pleading. Pen goes to her desk and it is a relief for her to have something to do, to have a focus that is Alice and also not Alice.

'I have paper?'

But Alice's hands are already busy with her phone. Alice looks up. Alice presses the green arrow.

And then Pen's phone beeps. Pen takes the two steps to the bed and picks it up, presses the button to take her to Alice's message. And then Pen reads something she did not know:

I DON'T LIKE ANYONE. NOT IN THAT WAY.

Pen is silent. Pen looks at the screen. Pen reads it and rereads it. She knows what it means, and she also does not know. Like she is looking at the words, but she has forgotten how to read.

'You don't like me.' Statement, not question.

Pen can't look at Alice, can't see what her face is doing, wouldn't know what it meant anyway. Another beep from her phone.

I LIKE YOU. I LIKE YOU SO MUCH. BUT I DON'T FEEL ANYTHING.

Pen looks up. Alice's eyes are shining, and her face is white. Now Alice speaks:

'I like the idea of it. Or, I think I do. When girls would talk, you know, about boys and touching them or whatever, I thought "ugh", because I always thought I liked girls. But then with girls too, it's like the things that other people say or pictures or whatever online. They don't *mean* anything. I can't imagine, I can't imagine . . .'

Alice stops.

Pen, who knows what it is like to get stuck, to be looking at the same thing as everyone else but to see something completely different, says, 'I know.' Even though she does not.

'It's like the bit that connects looking to feeling doesn't, like, work in me.' Alice looks at Pen.

Pen thinks about how Alice sent this message to her.

'I'm sorry. I have no one else to tell.'

Pen hears Alice say this, and she does not move.

'I tried to tell my parents that I feel *different* to everyone else, but they're not, they're not like Claire, they just make me keep a diary of my feelings, as if it doesn't really matter.'

Pen is in her body and she says to her body, to her brain, do something.

'But you touched me.' Pen moves her head, towards the bed, and is there again, Alice's arms around her, fingertips on her.

But Alice is shaking her head. 'I thought, if I tried. If I tried, I could be like other people. I just . . .' And Alice's eyes are leaking, her shoulders up, arms around herself, 'I'm so stupid.'

Pen breathes. In and out. Alice-does-not-want-her. But no, that was not the right answer. Because it's not that Alice does not want her, it's that Alice does not want anyone.

Alice says, 'I think it's called Ace.'

And Pen nods again.

'Like, being asexual . . . But, like, I don't even know, like saying that word, I don't even know if that's me. Like, maybe it's something I'll grow out of, maybe I'm just a late developer?'

And Pen knows this thought so well. That somehow this thing inside you, this thing that makes you different, will just go away.

Alice is not Alice. Or not the Alice Pen thought she was, not *her* Alice.

But Alice is definitely still Alice. Also true.

Pen wants to howl because she will never be with her now.

But Alice is in her room. Alice is with her.

Pen looks down at her phone, at her hands holding the phone.

Breathe.

Message. New.

Breathe.

Type.

Breathe.

And she hesitates for a second because even written down, words are hard.

Send.

Turn and face Alice, who you love.

Alice's face.

Alice's tears on her face.

She is reading Pen's text.

It is everything Pen knows and thinks and feels and it is not an answer to Alice's question, but it is all she can think to give.

Because this is what love looks like in real life.

YOU ARE ENOUGH.

11.07 pm

Aidan dumps the final dregs of dinner into the compost, and a little slops out. He rips a sheet of kitchen roll off and bends to wipe the side of the bin. Might as well change the bag. Ruth never bothers with the bins, she would live in a house with overflowing rubbish if he let her. Aidan's father is the same. His dad couldn't seem to learn the knack of housework, how things that had been done by his wife now had to be done by him. It had been easier in the end to hire a cleaning woman, though his dad pretends to hate it. 'She moves my things,' he grumbles each week. 'That's her job, Dad,' Aidan says. It's cold outside now, and Aidan hurries to the end of the garden, lifts the brown lid, drops the bag in. Still fairly empty. The lid bangs closed behind him.

'What do we do now?' Ruth had asked.
    'Keep talking, I guess,' Aidan said. 'Go to counselling.'
    'Work out where we go from here.'
    'Something like that, Ruth.'

All his childhood, Aidan's father would never express pride, that was the thing. 'I am not responsible,' he would say, 'all the credit goes to my son.' So it was out of character, at their engagement dinner, when he had asked for some quiet. He had spoken of watching his son play as a child, in a sandpit now long gone. He had watched Aidan patiently adding sand to the bucket, upending it, tapping the top. Saw that each castle was a personal triumph, that each turret that crumbled was a deeply felt loss. He spoke of how he had kept watching as Aidan did not flatten the broken ones, but went on, as was his habit, with the next. 'That was when,' he said, 'I knew my son would be a man of integrity.' And then, the most unlikely thing, his father had recited, 'Twinkle, twinkle, little star, now they know how bright you are. Was I surprised? Well, don't you know – I saw you shining long ago.' And Aidan had been amazed. So much so, that he had spoiled the moment, and instead of thanking his father, he had asked him if he'd found the rhyme in a Christmas cracker.

Aidan locks the back door behind him, drops the keys in the dish on the shelf. 'When are you two going to give me grandkids?' his father had started asking right after the wedding, enjoying their blushes. Then had come the clinics and the treatments, and his dad knew enough to stop asking. But a while ago, it had slipped out, something about how they'd understand the bigger picture when they had kids. There had been a pause, as they all registered the mistake. Then instead of redirecting or shrugging it off as she usually did, Ruth had wept. 'No, no, no, no,' she had sobbed, over and over. And Aidan's father had nodded, then put his hand on Ruth's shoulder. She had resisted for a moment, before turning to lean on her father-in-law. 'It's alright now,' he had said, patting Ruth's back and looking over her head. He met Aidan's eye with such clear sorrow that both men had quickly looked away. 'It's alright now,' he repeated. And Aidan had stood by, watching his wife and his father, wanting someone to comfort him.

11.08 pm

Alice is still looking at her phone screen, because it's too hard to look at Pen. And there is a tiny gap, where she can hear them both breathing, or maybe she can hear them both holding their breath. Pen shuffles a bit, and Alice thinks, I have to keep going.

'I'm so sorry about tonight and leaving you in town. I wanted to tell you so many times, just the words wouldn't come.' Alice pauses because it is hard to say to your best friend that you worried she would think you were weird, and that maybe she would say all the mean things to you that would hurt you. And it is especially hard when you kind-of-okay-definitely-do-know that your best friend wants to kiss you. Alice hopes Pen doesn't think that she was always lying.

Pen's mother knocks on the door. 'Don't make me be the mean mother,' she says, and Alice and Pen smile and it is the first smile since Alice said, 'Ace.'

'Okay,' says Pen, which is mostly what she says, and they listen as Claire goes back downstairs.

'I'm sorry that I'm not . . .' Alice stops.

'Do you have . . .' Pen begins. 'Do you ever want to, with anyone?'

Alice shakes her head, and it's easier to talk now. 'It's like, when I try to imagine it, two people together, it's like

233

neither of them is me. As if I'm looking on, and one of them is called Alice, and she kind of looks like me, but it can't be me. Not me in my own body. Maybe that's what a meltdown is like?'

Pen shrugs and nods at the same time.

'And I, god, this is so embarrassing, but I like get hot and stuff, you know, down there, and it's okay if I touch myself. But if someone else touches me, it feels really weird, like not my body. Because I don't want them to.'

'Okay,' Pen says, and then, 'I think that's normal, actually.'

'Yeah. But remember that party?' Alice stops for a second, because Pen never comes to parties. 'Anyway, there was that solstice party or whatever and there was this guy there and everyone said we would be, like, perfect together. But I left the party early and then everyone wrote things like "Tease" on my profile and stuff.'

Pen nods but doesn't say anything, and actually this is one of the reasons Alice likes being with her, she doesn't try to talk over you. Alice feels really tired suddenly, and kind of old. She takes a step towards Pen. 'Pen? Do you think it would be okay if we hugged?'

Pen looks like she's not going to do anything. And then she nods.

Alice takes another step forwards and puts her arms around Pen.

Pen is warm and strong. Alice feels the tiredness leave her.

Pen puts her arms around Alice, and it is like how she imagined it would be. And it is completely different. Pen thinks of Claire, of what she had said when Pen asked her was she disappointed in having her as a daughter. 'Oh, Pen. You don't always get the thing you wanted,' Claire had whispered, smiling and crying, 'Sometimes you get something else instead.'

Alice is like a bird in Pen's arms, like a bundle of twigs, like a bag of feathers.

Alice is in Pen's arms.

Ruth eyes herself in the mirror, shifting her weight to one leg, so she only sees half of her face, that's better. It is just as well, she thinks, that you can't see yourself when you're crying because you'd only cry harder. Ruth has the feeling she gets after fights, of being wounded, of having said too much, of wanting to take it all back. And of release, too. I am open now, she thinks.

Love is so unlikely a thing, can you say that you are still *in love* with someone after all this time, can you love someone after they have hurt you so deeply? Ruth puts toothpaste on a toothbrush with splayed bristles. I will never be a mother, she says to her reflection, but begins brushing before there can be an answer. She is just herself, there's no one else she can be. She bends and spits into the basin, rinses with water from the tap, looks up again at the mirror. And it is her mother's voice she hears: 'Did you think it would all be plain sailing?'

Ruth listens to the click from downstairs, it must be Aidan turning off the hall light. Yes, there are his feet on the stairs. Pass me by, don't pass me by. She holds her breath as he reaches the bathroom door, but he turns on the half-landing, goes up the next flight, into their bedroom, and she hears another click. The bedside light. Ruth pictures him looking at their room, his still-packed case leaning against the chest of drawers, the unmade bed. There, the rasp of the curtains being pulled.

Ruth flicks off the light and shuts the bathroom door softly. Hesitates on the landing. She will not join him just yet.

Through the box-room window, she sees the street lamp's yellow glow refracted through the tree, a pattern of light and dark. Opposite, she sees the roof of the park keeper's cottage, the mesh of the tennis-court fence, hedges and parked cars. The road has a sheen to it as if it had rained while they were arguing, drowning, saving themselves.

There is a clatter on the stairs, but it is not their house, it is one of the children next door, up late, or perhaps a parent hurrying up the stairs to check on them.

Ruth could have walked away, she still could. But every time she has heard her own voice today, reverberating in her mind – *run*, *stay* – she has stayed, has advanced, has chosen dependence after all.

There is another noise from the bedroom, but still Ruth hesitates. She needs one more minute. One more minute to look out the window, to see the way the shadows fall on the street outside. One more minute to contemplate all the shadows that fall inside the house too. One more minute to just be.

And when that minute is up, she will go in to him. She will go to her husband, and she will put her hand on his chest, skin to skin. And if he does not shrink from her, if he looks at her, or touches her back, then she will lean in to him and say, I know what I want. Let's be us again.

11.53 pm

It's late.

Pen does not know the time, or exactly how long it is since Alice went downstairs. How long since they held each other.

Claire sees the light around the edge of the door, pushes it a little further open. Pen is sixteen, but she is still her baby girl.

'Is Alice okay?' her mum asks, and Pen nods because it's too complicated, even though it's also simple, simple to see now. The 'big blues' Alice got sometimes. The fear that crossed her face when a boy or girl came too close. The being at the centre but always saying she felt outside.

Claire steps into the room. 'Are you guys just friends, or can I ask . . . ?'

Pen's throat burns. A small shake. Alice is not *her* Alice, but that is not Pen's story to tell.

'She likes me as a friend,' Pen says.

'Here, shove over.' Pen's mother squeezes onto the bed with her and she is not looking at her, just shoulders touching, which is okay.

'Oh, Pen, I know it might not feel like it, but a best friend is the most important relationship of your life.'

Claire pauses and Pen knows her mother is going to say something else.

'If you want to talk, or anything,' Claire pauses, 'I mean, talking is better than cutting—'

'Mum!'

'Sorry, Pen, it's just it's okay—'

'I'm not going to do that!'

'Well, that's good to hear. No judgement, Pen.'

And it is funny-strange, because the idea of cutting again hadn't even come into her head. Pen feels a kind of calm. The plan didn't work out, but love was maybe like that. The house clicks and is silent, click quiet, click quiet, all around them.

Claire rubs Pen's knee through the duvet. 'That allowed?'

Pen nods because it is more than okay. Something inside Pen, her heart, eases. And she wishes she could give this feeling to Alice too.

'I'm proud of you, Pen. Because love is scary, and you took the risk anyway.'

'Okay,' Pen says.

'Well, then, time for sleep. Not all of us are teenagers with endless energy.'

Pen listens to Claire's voice. It is brisk again, and the notes are warm and kind. Which means everything is going to be alright.

11.55 pm

They have done this so many hundreds of times before. Ruth walks two steps towards her husband, and in the quiet she hears his breathing, heavy, like he is lifting something. It is so familiar, so precise, the way she puts her hand on his chest, rubs with one finger. He shifts his head slightly, she draws hers in, their lips meet, it is almost obscene, this act of a kiss. Aidan's lips part and her tongue goes into his mouth, how strange a ritual, Ruth thinks, as she strokes her tongue against his. A kiss.

Without willing it, his hips push towards her. Aidan wonders how long it is since they did this, since they wanted each other. Wait, he might say, wait. Ruth pulls her shirt up and he watches her skin reveal itself, wants, suddenly, to put his lips to that soft, exposed plane. His fingers tremble.

Ruth unclasps her bra. Perhaps it is too fast, too much. Wait, she might say, wait. But her hands keep moving, her body pulling towards his. Aidan is reaching out to touch her. As they begin to make love, Ruth thinks, this is wonderful, but the words don't stay in her mind, and don't mean what she wants them to anyway.

'Hello,' Aidan says, his face on the pillow next to her. He gently pushes a strand of hair out of her eyes.

'Hello,' Ruth says. 'That was good?'

'Yeah,' Aidan lets out a long exhale, his eyes closing briefly. 'Christ, I'm wiped now, though.'

He pulls the duvet up over them, concealing the evidence, and Ruth smiles to herself at this man who has always hated talking after sex. 'Long day,' she allows herself to say.

'Yeah.'

Ruth looks over at him, his eyes closed properly now. 'I might get some water, want some?'

'No, I'm grand.'

The house feels different as she walks through it. Hospitable again, maybe. Back in the bedroom, Ruth stands in the door for a moment, watching Aidan. He is asleep, like someone with a clear conscience. *Don't dwell, Ruth. Just let it be how it is.*

It isn't easy, though, it has never been easy, letting people be the way they wanted with you. Ruth slides into bed, thinking of the ceremony and the words they'd written, of the hope and perfection, of how he had looked at her. And how he had kept his eyes closed tonight as they'd made love. He fucks me, he fucks me not, he fucks me. Sex, Ruth thinks as she settles onto the pillow, sex could not fix it all. But it had meant something. Downstairs he said she had abandoned him. And yet here they are and there is nowhere else and there is no other time and there is no other person.

It was their favourite joke from the beginning, that Aidan looked after her, fed her, cherished and minded her, but Ruth had not wanted it, she sees now, to be only a joke. He had been shocked, his face had betrayed him, shocked to hear her say that she grieved too. If you don't know that, she wanted to say, you are not paying attention, not minding me at all. She is so tired of it now, of revolving it all, and she shifts slightly away from him. Aidan sighs and turns to curve round her, then breathes deeply again. He had not paid attention. But then neither had she.

Aidan didn't get it, or not fully, that Ruth's work was not so much a consolation as a way of making something new. Something that was both outside herself and that came from inside. It's hard to express, exactly, but she wants it for herself, and she wants, too, to come home to Aidan, to talk it over, share it with him, all of it. Because she has not heard or felt or seen anything until she has told Aidan. And this is the revelation of today, though it is a fact that has been there all along: the only way forward for her is to be in this completely. No more running away.

Ruth feels so close to him now, his breathing gentle, whispering up against her neck. She will have a family. Even if family is in a different shape than she thought it would be.

What had she said to that girl, earlier? Name one thing you can see? Ruth looks at the outline of the curtains and the wardrobe, and thinks, this is my life. Name one thing you can feel? The duvet wrapped around my legs. My life settling around me. Name one thing you can touch? Aidan, at last. Aidan.

A future.

The clock shows nearly one am. They will never move on, she sees, either of them. They will just learn to carry it. To deal with it, one bit, then another bit. This is what it is to build a life with another person. How weird, how hard. When will it not be hard? Never, but do it anyway. Ruth is getting tired, but she doesn't want to lose this moment, to let it end.

Ruth is not easy, who wants easy, he is not easy either.

Someone else would be easier, she will say that to him, tomorrow, wait until he's had breakfast, and coffee, definitely coffee, and say it to him, did you want easy, did you, because I wanted interesting, and we can still be interesting, can't we? They have found an armistice, not a resolution, and tomorrow they will do it all again and come up with better answers and different truths and find a path or a way through and it is not all gone, it is not too late, there is still time.

What was the question?

Is this what you want?

In the dark, breathing soft now, hope and love and kindness and acceptance. Is this what you want? In the dark but also in the light. Is this what you want?

Yes, she thinks, yes, it is. Yes.

1.15 am

No girls kissing.

'Could you still be my girlfriend,' Alice had said at the end, 'if I don't want to have sex?' And Pen hadn't really answered because she did not want to seem like she only wanted Alice for one thing. But Pen likes girls, she wants real sex with a girl, and she holds this truth inside her.

Pen wonders if it is the same way for Alice, of feeling like being different makes you dangerous. She remembers her mother and father talking about her, using words like over-sensitive and syndrome and diagnosis. Her mother had taken her for all those tests, insisting and pushing and getting called difficult by the GP and the headmistress, until Claire said she understood what Pen went through. Sometimes Sandy would look at her, would forget and try to touch her face, like he was checking she was actually there, and when Pen pulled away, he would shake his head. And then there were the fights and the slamming, and Pen screaming and Lauren's house and the razor, and Claire sobbing and Sandy sitting in his car, crying, with his head on the wheel.

So now they live here, and Pen goes to a normal school where she is not normal, but she is herself, and her mother is herself too and her sister is really good at art, but can't sleep without a nightlight, and gets so stressed about school and seeing her father that she vomits sometimes. Pen's mother says she'll never love again, cackling but also crying on the phone to her best friend, Lisa, who's just had a baby, who is worried about being old, who will be over sixty when the kid's still-in-school-for-god's-sake. And Alice, the most popular girl in their class, is Ace.

There is no normal, so this is normal.

Pen thinks of Alice sleeping downstairs, the sheets and duvet, the sag in the middle, the glow of the clock on the DVD, the noise of the fridge which you can hear at night, the ticking from cooling radiators, maybe a car going by, slowing for the lights. But maybe Alice is asleep, her breathing easy and regular. Pen hopes so, Pen hopes she can sleep soft and deep. Had she said or done the right things for Alice? She will think of better words tomorrow, tomorrow the words will come, tomorrow she will listen.

Pen turns onto her side, closing her eyes, sliding her hand between her legs, pressing her face into the pillow. And thinks of what she did not say. Of how she had wanted to cry out, 'I just wanted to love you, like other people.' But her mum was right, and it is enough, for now, that Pen is not alone, that her best friend is here, and there will be other kinds of love. Pen's shoulders relax a little. Tomorrow. Pen is not sure about tomorrow, but today has been enough. She whispers a word, *libera*, the syllables velvety, hopeful in her mouth.

Pen begins to rub. The material of her pyjamas is thin, and she can feel her fingers' warmth as she touches herself, gently at first. The cotton bunches and so she slips her hand under the waistband. Her heart starts to beat a little faster and it always feels like this, so many things to think of, pick one, focus on one. Pen's palm is smooth against her as she moves it down, catching a little wetness on her fingers. Her middle finger begins to probe. To circle, round and round. Direct, don't re-direct, okay, Pen, you know how to do this. Pen feels the melt begin, as she slides a finger inside. A second's pressure, now two inside, twisting in the wet. This is her body. Her pleasure. Her wanting. All hers. She feels it in those fingers first, a contraction, then a spasm that ripples through her.

Here she is.

ACKNOWLEDGEMENTS

Simon Prosser believed in this book from the start. My sincere thanks to him for his enthusiasm and generosity, and to Hermione Thompson, Anna Ridley, Leah Boulton and all at Hamish Hamilton. My thanks also to Karolina Sutton and Molly Atlas for their friendship and expert guidance, and to the entire team at Curtis Brown. For their insights on writing about autism, my thanks to Jody O'Neill and Eleanor Walsh. This book was begun while I was writer-in-residence at the National Maternity Hospital and my thanks to all there. Returning to my academic job during Covid has made me even more grateful than usual for all my wonderful colleagues, and our students, in the School of English, Drama and Film at University College Dublin.

To my family of friends, a heartfelt thank you. For specific moments of writing advice, particular thanks to John Butler, Anna Carey, Alex Marrable, Tony Roche and Pádraic Whyte.

Thank you to my sister, Vanessa, for the joy, wisdom and strength she brings. And thank you to my parents, Melanie and Richard, for all that they have given me, and for always being their brilliant selves.

This book is for Ronan, again and always.